TWISTED LOYALTIES

KNIGHTS OF THE TWISTED TREE
BOOK TWO

BARBARA J. WEBB

TWISTED LOYALTIES

Book Two of KNIGHTS OF THE TWISTED TREE

Copyright © 2024 by Barbara J. Webb

Book Cover Design by ebooklaunch.com

Cover art copyright © 2023

All rights reserved.

ISBN 978-0-9675066-5-4

To the lonely

$\mathcal{K}$ ORIN HAD LEARNED to live with nightmares. It had taken only a few days on the warfront for them to start, and they'd been a part of his life ever since.

The voices were always the same. The screams, the sobs, the moans. People in pain, suffering. Korin could hear them, could see them, could stand among them, but he could never help. Every time he tried, every time he reached out to touch, they would crumble and blow away like ashes on the wind.

So he walked across the blood-soaked battlefield. On the earth scorched black by fire and magic. Through people who were twitching piles of scorched flesh, others who had been literally torn apart, people with sword wounds and axe wounds, with crushed bones and caved skulls, drowning in pools of their own blood. All crying out to him. Begging. Pleading. For help. For release.

Korin could do nothing.

At the center of it all stood a tree. Bare. Twisted. Dead. Under a moonless sky, it cast its shadow over the dead, reaching fingers of gnarled darkness that touched each and every body. As Korin walked towards the tree, those same shadows criss-crossed his own body, scratched at his skin, caught in his hair.

A tendril of shadow reared up at Korin's approach, resolving into an enormous snake, pale as a ghost. It oozed the decaying energy of the blight. Korin met its silver serpent eyes. The snake, she—for it was a she—slid down the tree and onto Korin's outstretched arm.

They suffer. The snake spoke in Korin's mind. The voice of the knife, the voice of the tree. The voice of death.

Korin stood still as the snake wrapped around him, settling her weight across his shoulders and around his waist. All the while, his attention was on the battlefield, on the tortured, the dying. "I can't help them."

The snake responded to the sadness in Korin's voice, rubbed her head against his face. Her scales were warm and surprisingly soft. **We can help them. You and I. Together.**

Korin knew it was wrong. The snake—the tree—they couldn't help. They could only destroy. The blight, it was worse than anything the people on the battlefield suffered. And yet... and yet...

There's nothing to fear. You love these people, and so do I.

"No," Korin whispered. "You don't love them. You torture them. You kill them."

The serpent stroked his face again, a gentle touch, despite the prickling cold of the blight. **They don't understand. They fear my power, but that makes it no less a gift.** The serpent's tail wound around Korin's arm, lifting it with irresistible strength. **Show them, Korin. Show them my love. Show them yours.**

Power flowed from Korin's hand, life and death twined together. His power, the tree's power, merged as one. It spread across the field, a cloud of energy that left silence everywhere it touched.

Korin tried to stop it, tried to close his hand, but he couldn't. He opened his mouth to scream, but the snake darted in, filling his mouth, his throat. Its power moved over him, through him, the blight eating away at him from the inside.

Dragging him down into darkness.

"Hold still. This won't hurt. I promise." Korin gave his best reassuring smile to the terrified little girl. He looked up at the girl's mother who wore a similarly stricken look as she held her daughter tight as she could while allowing Korin access to the girl's broken arm.

This was a greenstick break, fresh and clean. The bone hadn't pushed through the skin, and the mother had known to bring the girl straight away to Korin. An easy fix.

Korin took the little girl's wrist in one hand and laid his other hand across the break as lightly as he could. He closed his eyes and focused, reaching into the arm with his magic. The first thing he did was pinch around the nerves at the little girl's shoulder to dull the pain.

The little girl gasped, and the shocked terror relaxed into sobbing tears. Korin worked fast while mother and daughter both were focused on her crying. The old shape of the arm was there. The bone remembered how it was supposed to be. Korin focused on that shape and fed a burst of energy into the girl's arm.

With an audible snap, the bone popped back into place, as solid and true as if it had never been broken. The little girl screeched with surprise and tried to jerk away, but Korin held tight to her wrist. He still needed to repair the rest of the damage, realign flesh and muscle and torn blood vessels back to where they should be. "Just a little bit more," he murmured, as soothing as he could manage from the half-trance of magic. "And then you'll be back to climbing trees."

Attuned to her body, Korin felt the chemical jolt of new fear at the mention of trees. Maybe she wouldn't be so quick to go climbing again. Which would be sad, if this trauma scarred her emotionally when Korin had made sure it wouldn't do so physically. But children were resilient and...wait.

There was something not quite right. What was it? An…echo, maybe. A twinge of something as Korin was searching for the arm as it had been, moving through the feel of the injury itself.

And now he was alert, he noticed other things. Like the fact the girl had no bruising anywhere else on her body. If she'd fallen out of a tree, as she'd claimed, there should be some amount of injury elsewhere, even if it was only superficial.

Korin's first worried thought was that someone had broken the girl's arm—an abuse she was afraid to say. Except that would leave bruising too. Maybe not visible, but Korin would be able to see the broken capillaries and crushed skin from hands gripping too tight or a sudden blow.

No, it was as if this girl's arm had just snapped all on its own. With no outside force marking her skin in any other way. Which wasn't possible.

Unless that strange little echo Korin felt was magic. Someone else's magic. Another wizard had done this.

"All better," Korin said, opening his eyes. As he let go, he released the nerves so the girl could feel again. If he'd done his job right—and he had—there would be nothing left to cause her pain.

The little girl was still crying, but now had both her arms wrapped around her mother, giving no sign that either one was causing her any trouble. "Thank you," the mother said, sincere, but awkward. She couldn't meet Korin's eyes, and was already gathering herself to stand.

Because once he was done healing them, they always remembered he was a wizard.

Korin was used to it. He stood, giving her the polite excuse to do the same. The woman was definitely nervous of him, and the little girl was still terrified. And maybe there was nothing unusual about that, or maybe… "Can I ask…did you see her fall?"

The mother shook her head, and her eyes slid away from Korin's, guilty and afraid. Korin didn't know what to make of it and when he said nothing else, the woman lifted her daughter and left without another word, winding her way around the chairs and tables that filled the bar side of the guesthouse.

Since the bar wasn't open yet, Marta—the guesthouse's owner —let Korin use the room to deal with anyone who came to him for help. It was quieter than the always-busy kitchen and meant Korin didn't have to take strangers up to his room.

Korin had been here not-quite a month and word of his presence was spreading through the neighborhood—through the whole city. People were getting to know his skill as a healer and—more importantly—the fact he gave his magic away for free, unlike the Wing wizards who lived in the nicer parts of town and charged more money per healing than Korin had ever seen in his life.

Korin stretched. This morning had been a busy one. In addition to the little girl, he'd seen three men with injuries that had gotten infected, an old woman with a broken hip, and a boy with a stomach virus Korin was going to have to keep an eye out for in case it spread. A solid morning's work.

Korin had never stayed in one place for this long. It was a little scary to think that he was gaining a reputation, that people were learning his name.

He turned to see Verania standing in the door that led back to the kitchen. She wore a bright smile on her pretty face and held a steaming bowl of chicken and rice in her hands. "Thought you might be hungry after all that."

Korin returned her smile. The upside of lingering in one place —friends. People who cared who he was and how he was. People he could like. People he could trust. "Thanks, Verania."

She brought him the food, made him sit back down, went back to the kitchen to find him something to drink. All the girls who worked here liked to fuss over him. Marta, too, in her own surly way. It made Korin feel like he belonged. It made him feel like he was home.

Verania returned with a tall glass of pineapple juice, which was Korin's current favorite. "Anything else you need?" she asked.

Korin smiled and shook his head. Verania gave a wink and a twirl, making her bright skirts swirl wide as she left. Flirting. Not seriously. Marta had made it clear from the first day Korin had moved in that she didn't approve of fraternizing.

Not that Korin would have been interested. Not in the girls. And besides, he had someone.

Maybe. Sort of.

Korin couldn't hold back his smile when he thought of Ádan. Handsome Ádan with his bright grins and irrepressible cheer. Dangerous Ádan with his secrets and his oaths to people Korin didn't know how to trust. Ádan who had saved Korin's life, but in doing so, had pulled Korin into the middle of a horrible secret Korin didn't know if he could face.

Ádan who had now been away for two weeks, summoned by Prince Lysander zhi Ritalle to join the prince in his entourage. Lysander had been in Ulek, at the war front, but he wanted his friend next to him on the journey home. As Ádan had apologetically reported to Korin before riding off.

Korin missed him. Korin didn't miss him. Korin wanted him back right now. Korin thought it might be better if he never saw Ádan again.

But mostly, Korin filled his days with helping the people who came to him. There'd been no sense obsessing when Ádan was away and Korin couldn't do anything about it.

Now Korin had a new question to worry about—what *had* happened to that little girl? Was he imagining things, or...was it possible a wizard had done that? If so, why? And who?

Korin finished his food, took the dishes back to the kitchen, then stuck his head into Marta's office. She sat at her desk, working her way through a ledger, a woman of unguessable age with greying black hair and a will of iron. "What is it, Korin?" she asked without looking up.

"You need anything from me today?"

She stopped with a finger on the last line she'd been studying, looked up at him, considering. "No, I think we're good. You going out?"

"I was going to go to the parade."

She grunted, dismissive of the whole idea. "Go on with you. You got money?"

"Enough. I'll be fine."

She grunted again and returned her attention to the book. Finished with him.

Korin was out the door before anyone else could show up to stop him.

CROWDS HAD ALREADY gathered along the parade route. It seemed like everyone in Triome had turned up. Korin had never seen so many people all in one place. On the streets, packed into balconies, at windows, along rooftops.

Smells of spicy chicken and roasting cinnamon made Korin's stomach rumble, despite that he'd just eaten. The food in Triome had been a revelation, and Korin had yet to stop being amazed by it.

Korin squeezed through the back of the crowd, moving up the street, but couldn't find any gaps offering a good vantage point. It hadn't occurred to him there would be this many people. It hadn't occurred that there *could* be this many people.

Something stung his neck, and Korin slapped reflexively. The insects here were another new thing, although most of the time they ignored him. Except there wasn't anything there. Korin was lowering his hand just as something small and hard struck his knuckle. This time, he saw the pebble bounce away as it fell. Then a third struck his shoulder.

Korin looked around. Was someone throwing rocks at him?

But no one seemed to be paying him any attention. His eyes scanned the crowd. He looked all around. Then up.

Two buildings down, on the second story roof of a manor walled off from the street, was a face Korin recognized. A handsome, firstborn face on a solid, warrior's body. One of the knights, although not the one Korin most wanted to see.

Varajas waved, beckoning Korin to join him on the roof.

Getting there proved an interesting challenge. There were no obvious places to climb the wall that existed to keep people out of the gardens surrounding this house. Korin had to run and jump, catching the top of the wall with his fingertips, and scrabble up before he lost his grip. He crept nervously through the lush green garden, certain he wasn't supposed to be there. A sturdy trellis got him to the top of the first story, and from there he had to ease along a narrow eave to reach the part of the second story roof that sloped down low enough to grab, then pull himself up again.

A few weeks ago, Korin wouldn't have been able to do this. He'd been ragged, exhausted, first from hard travel and war, and then from a brutal encounter with destructive magic. But time healed all wounds, especially when one was a wizard like Korin. A few quiet weeks of rest and recovery, coupled with the steamy Spring weather and as much delicious food as he could eat and Korin was in possibly the best shape of his life.

Varajas waited for Korin, nodded as Korin carefully crossed the central peak, then worked his way down the slope to join him. Varajas wore a light cloth wrap around his head, protection from the sun, but also a convenient way to hide his face. He'd pulled the cloth back up over his nose, so only his eyes were visible.

"Were you throwing rocks at me?" Korin asked as he sat down.

"Got your attention."

In truth, Korin was surprised Varajas had wanted him up here at all. It wasn't like they were friends. Korin knew the knights' secrets—the most important of which being the fact that they still existed at all. The rest of the world thought they were dead, defeated two months ago in Ulek, at the end of a war that still gave Korin nightmares. But Varajas, along with Ádan and Nikki had escaped the final blows and made it to Triome, dragging a horrible, dangerous burden along with them.

"You're looking better," Varajas commented.

The last time Varajas had seen Korin had been at the end of a fight against monsters who had almost taken Korin's life. Varajas, Ádan, and Nikki had saved Korin. "I never got a chance to thank you—"

Varajas waved away Korin's thanks. "It's a nice day. No reason to talk about that."

Korin couldn't argue. The bright afternoon sun was tempered by the cool, salty breeze coming in off the ocean. Up here, neither the noise nor the smell of the crowds below was overwhelming. Korin had a fleeting regret that he hadn't stopped to grab some of the cinnamon almonds a vendor below was selling, fresh roasted and fragrant, but it wasn't worth climbing back down to get them.

Cheers rippled through the crowd as the leading edge of the parade came into view. Acrobats in bright flowing silks leaped and tumbled, graceful and colorful as exotic birds. "Oh," Korin breathed.

Varajas snorted. "Don't get out much, do you?"

"I've never seen anything like this." Most of Korin's life had been spent in small, remote towns and villages in the freezing south. Or the small, remote school where he'd learned to be a wizard. Or at war.

"This is just the warm-up," Varajas said. "Getting the crowd excited so they'll cheer properly for the people who matter."

Korin didn't know what to say to that, so he just kept watching. After the acrobats came music, flutes and drums and pipes, and behind the musicians, dancers draped in flashing crystal jewelry and little else.

More acrobats and a man breathing fire. An army of dancers in bright feathers. A flame wizard surrounded by twirling women whose bodies sparked with illusionary fire as they moved.

It was all magic to Korin.

The cheers of the crowd swelled to a roar as the first riders came around a bend in the street. "Behold the conquering heroes," Varajas muttered, bitter.

At the front of the line, bejeweled and glamorous, as if they had appeared out of some legend, riding side by side on prancing horses of matching black, Archduke Rhanis zhi Darkivel and his daughter, Archwizard Sheluna of the Wing. Their golden hair flowed bright in the tropical sun as they waved at their cheering audience. The Archduke was old, over one hundred and fifty years, but firstborn aged slowly and gracefully, and he more resembled some fabled warrior prince than a man nearing the end of his prime. Sheluna was a wizard—was the Archwizard—of the only order that knew as much about shaping the body as did Korin's own. Which meant she was exactly as beautiful as she wanted to be, and what she clearly wanted to be was breathtaking. Both were dressed in striking blacks, shining gold, and the dark, rich sapphire color that was known from south to north as Darkivel blue.

The Darkivels. The heroes who had tirelessly led ten years of brutal warfare to save the world from the demonic scourge of the knights, their Grandmaster, and their King.

"I hate them," Varajas whispered.

Korin didn't know what to think. The world, as he was learning, was more complicated than he had ever realized in his time spent on the warfront dealing with the results of the vicious tactics both sides had leveraged.

Behind the Darkivels rode a man with iron-gray hair, dressed in silver-threaded black. Korin didn't recognize the man's face, but he knew the meaning of the twin swords at the man's hips and the Prophet's cross hanging from his neck. "Is that High Father Donatien?"

"Of course it is," Varajas answered. "Who else would be riding with the snakes?"

Korin flinched at the word *snake*, and shivered under the hot afternoon sun. He glanced at Varajas, but V's attention was still on the parade. He didn't seem to have meant anything significant. Nor had he noticed Korin's reaction. Korin looked back down at Donatien, leader of the Bladed Brothers, the militant arm of the church.

Korin had seen plenty of Blades on the warfront. He'd kept his distance, as had any wizard with sense. The Brothers had been there to fight against the knights, but they specialized in killing the gifted, whether those gifted were wizard-knights or order-sworn wizards. Donatien and all his followers were on good terms with Archwizard Sheluna, which should have meant they were harmless to any wizard who kept their oath, but there were whispers. There were always whispers.

An ordered column of Blades rode behind their High Father, pulling a "Shit," out of Varajas.

"What?"

Varajas shook his head. "Nothing. Just…Blades in the city. Could be trouble."

Something in Varajas's voice sounded off, but before Korin could ask another question, he was distracted.

Behind the Blades, a completely different group. Dressed in bright colors, their horses prancing and sidestepping with restless energy, the vivid opposite of the tight, disciplined column they followed. Korin's stomach gave a flip as he recognized one of them. "Is that Ádan?"

Varajas rolled his eyes. "Of course it is," he said with the same flat disapproval as he'd expressed for High Father Donatien and the Darkivels.

"He's back." Korin couldn't keep the excitement out of his voice.

"Along with the prince." Varajas pointed at the man to Ádan's right. A firstborn in bright gold mail on a bright gold horse, a flashing smile on his sharply handsome face as he waved to the crowd. "Lysander, the Darkivels, High Father Donatien, and Ádan. This city isn't big enough."

Korin was only half-listening. He couldn't take his eyes off Ádan. He looked like a prince himself. Dressed in silver and black leathers that molded perfectly to his muscular frame, Ádan stood tall in his stirrups, urging his horse to a prancing trot. He laughed in response to one of his companions, and Korin couldn't hold back his own answering smile.

Varajas sighed. "I'll see you around, Korin." He slipped away over the rooftop. Korin hardly noticed.

Ádan was back.

---

*Á*DAN LEANED OVER the railing of Prince Lysander's balcony, stared down at the woman wandering through the garden below, and tried not to think about just how much he hated her.

The Ritalle Royal Palace was a sprawling collection of golden-domed buildings and towers, loosely connected by lattice-covered walkways and tiled paths through the lush gardens that filled the in-between spaces. Lysander's tower was one of the tallest, a stone's throw from the Grand Gallery where the Queen-Regent held court, and Lysander's apartment was at the top, offering a spectacular view. A view which, at this moment, was ruined by the presence of Sheluna zhi Darkivel.

"Come inside, Ádan. Stop plotting to drop things on my mother's guests."

With one final wish for unspecified calamity to befall her, Ádan did as instructed.

The entire tower belonged to Lysander. Floor after floor was filled with every luxury imaginable, but this room at the top was Ádan's favorite. Open on all sides with wide, arching doorways and circled by balconies, magically shielded from weather and insects, and high enough that a person could forget the rest of the world existed.

The room itself was covered in soft carpet and deep cushions, with wind chimes at the corners offering a soft, gentle melody. Ádan could relax here. This was perhaps the one place left in all the world where he could feel at peace.

Lysander was here, draped across one of the man-sized pillows like some decadent sculptor's dream. Stripped of his golden mail, he was dressed casually in loose pants and a shirt cut open to the navel, exposing a wide expanse of flawless brown skin. In sprawling repose, he reminded Ádan of a jungle cat—all bundled energy, languid on the surface, but ready to strike. Spread with seemingly careless grace on the pillow, covered in lean, lithe muscles, every inch of himself was under perfect control at every moment. Lysander, the warrior-prince of Ritalle. Beloved of the people, acknowledged king-to-be. And now a hero of the war that had destroyed everything Ádan believed in and almost everyone he'd ever loved.

"How long are they staying?" Ádan asked, meaning the Darkivels.

"Mother is throwing a banquet tonight for Archduke Rhanis—which you're invited to, of course. She wants to formally acknowledge the great service he's done. But then I think he's gating back to Darkivel tomorrow."

"And Sheluna?"

"Lady Archwizard Sheluna zhi Darkivel of the Wing," Lysander drawled, "will be staying, a guest of the royal court. She told mother she had some project or another that's going to keep her in Ritalle for a while."

"Some project," Ádan repeated without inflection.

"That's what she said."

Sheluna zhi Darkivel had no business here. She'd never shown interest in the sort of research that went on at the School of the Balance—the wizard order headquartered here in the city. She'd never shown interest in anything that went on in the entirety of Ritalle.

Until now. And what a coincidence that Sheluna's new "project" in Triome was keeping her here just after the knife had been returned. The knife that had—for good or for ill—lived at the heart of the power of the order she had just destroyed. The knife that had only through the most desperate of efforts escaped her in Ulek.

Ádan might have been alarmed, if he hadn't pretty much used up all the energy he had for that already. "Well…fuck."

"Exactly."

Lysander knew the stakes, knew what Ádan had to protect. He was one of the only allies Ádan had left. But Lysander was as much a prisoner of his position as Ádan. They both had their obligations and their oaths.

Lysander had been in Ulek, fighting at Sheluna's side, because as the prince, that was his duty. To anyone observing, he'd been as staunch an enemy of the knights as anyone. But Lysander's presence, his careful leadership, had mitigated a great deal of pain and even saved a few lives. Just not the lives Ádan had most needed to see saved.

A body hanging from the broken gate, covered in carrion birds, eyes gone, skin ravaged.

"I hate her," Ádan said.

"She's a monster, no question. But you're not going to make her go away by standing on my balcony and glaring at her."

Which was true. Ádan needed a plan. A plan for how three surviving knights could protect the secret their entire order had been killed for. A plan for how to bind and control the knife when every person who had understood the knife's magic was dead. A plan for how to keep going when everything they believed in had been destroyed. "If you have a better suggestion, I'd love to hear it."

Lysander leaned back, staring up at the ceiling, his cool green eyes thoughtful. So many people underestimated him. They saw the Golden Prince with his wild reputation and wilder friends, who spent his days, not in the court where he belonged, but riding with the city guard or patrolling with the army, or hunting or gambling or various other irresponsible pursuits. So many people missed the keen, calculating mind that lurked behind Lysander's easy smile.

"I can't do anything about Ulek," Lysander said. "That's lost to you. And I can't make Sheluna unwelcome, much as I'd love to. But I can do one thing. There's going to be a council. I don't know when, but soon. Mother wants me to return to Ulek to speak for Ritalle. We don't know for sure you and V and Nikki are the only ones who escaped. I've got a few people I'd trust with this—to go looking for anyone else who made it out of Ulek at the end. Or who managed to not be there in the first place."

Ádan hadn't even thought about other survivors. Which was probably a sign he still wasn't thinking clearly.

A body swinging in the wind. Face pecked away, but the gleaming signet ring on his rotting hand made his identity unmistakable.

"I'd appreciate that," Ádan said. And then, "I should go check in with Nikki and V. Tell them…tell them what I saw."

"Be careful."

As if that were even possible anymore. "I'll see you soon."

ÁDAN HAD NEVER KNOWN the Academy as anything but a haunted ruin. Once upon a time, it had been beautiful, as grand as the Royal Palace or the School of the Balance. A tiny city all on its own, it had housed over a thousand knights, trainees, and allies. It had been wondrous.

That story ended before Ádan had been born.

Now the grounds and gardens were overgrown, the training fields choked with bushes and weeds. Beautifully carved stonework that had weathered hundreds of years without a sign of age was now crumbling. The grand hall, the barracks, the libraries, the schools, all collapsing in on themselves.

It wasn't a natural decay, and it would only speed and spread if Ádan didn't get good at his job fast.

In the center of the Academy, Ádan found the tree. Not everyone could see it. It wasn't real—not yet—merely a shadow of the power that lay in the underground deep below. But Ádan had touched the knife. He'd sworn the oath; the tree couldn't hide itself from him.

And that was the extent of the power Ádan was able to exert over it.

The shadow-tree reached up into the sky, its bare branches twisting around to block the sun no matter where Ádan stood. Ádan reached out to touch its black, rotting trunk, but his hand passed through the air because of course nothing was there.

"Talk to me," Ádan murmured. "Listen to me. You might as well. We're going to be together for a long time."

Silence. If the tree—the knife—truly had a voice, Ádan had yet to hear it.

Derian had talked about the knife's voice. How it—*she*, Derian always said *she*—had whispered to him, a constant companion in his ear, in his mind. Derian's faith in Ádan had been such that they'd only discussed the dangers of the whispered temptations and threats the knife could offer. He'd never considered the possibility that the knife might refuse to speak to Ádan at all.

"Are you angry?" Ádan was angry. "Are you lonely?"

Derian had taught Ádan as much as he could in the short time they had together. Ádan knew what the knife was—as much as Derian had. The truth of the knife—where it came from, who had made it—had been lost ages ago. All they knew was the power it held. Death, corruption, decay.

It couldn't be destroyed. Ádan knew that too. Generations of knights had tried. It could only be guarded, contained. And look where that had brought them.

"Do you miss him?" The knife had whispered to Derian, and Derian had talked back. Derian had spoken of the knife like she was—not a friend, exactly, but a companion. One with whom the relationship was complicated, but one he knew he'd never be free of.

Except in death.

"He's gone, but I'm sure you know that. I'm all you've got. You'll have to talk to me sooner or later. Or are you just going to sulk in your cave for the next hundred years?"

Footsteps rustling in the dead grass warned Ádan he wasn't alone. "Baby, don't be like that." Varajas's voice was gently mocking.

"Not helpful, V."

"Swear to God, Ádan, it was creepy enough when the Grandmaster would talk to that thing. Don't you start."

Varajas still didn't understand. Neither did Nikki. Ádan wasn't sure how to explain it to them. For the millionth time, he regretted how quickly they had to flee Ulek. If they'd had time for Derian to teach them the way he'd taught Ádan...

Ádan turned his back on the tree. He ignored the way he could still feel it like a cold breath on his neck, a whisper scratch across his back. Ignored the way it made his skin crawl.

Ignored the way the shadows changed. The fact that they were no longer empty, twisting branches. A new shadow stretched out before him, a shadow that looked exactly like a body hanging, swinging in the nonexistent breeze.

Ádan absolutely didn't turn around, didn't look. Didn't want to see if there was an actual body hanging there now, because he knew who that body would be. Instead, he started walking towards the Academy gate.

Varajas fell in beside him. "What did you see?" he asked.

Ádan experienced a brief moment of panic, thinking V was asking about the body in the tree. But after a pause, Varajas added, "In Ulek."

A creak from behind them—the sound of rope slipping and stretching. Ádan walked a little faster. "What do you want me to say? That everyone's dead? That it's going to be lifetimes before anything grows there again? That you can still smell the blood that's been ground into the dirt?"

"Ádan."

Ádan hated the soft tone of compassion. The last thing they needed right now was to start feeling sorry for each other. But all the same, it loosened something inside him, made him confess, "I saw *him*, V. Is that what you want to hear?"

Another creaking sound from behind. Exactly the same as Ádan had heard in Ulek. "They put magic on his body to keep it from rotting, but that didn't keep the birds away. They'd pecked out his eyes. His face was a mess. Unrecognizable." Except that Ádan would have known him anywhere. "It was just him, alone. Lysander talked the dukes into burying King Kolyn, but…" Ádan couldn't think what else to say.

And he did look back, because he couldn't help himself. Because he'd never in his life been someone who could simply not look.

Yes. There it was. Derian's body hung from the upper branches of the tree. It looked exactly as Ádan had seen it. Was the tree simply echoing his memories? Or was this a taunt, a gesture of cruelty?

Or worse, was this, in some strange way, the tree trying to make him feel better?

"We knew he was dead," Varajas said.

Yes, Ádan had known. But knowing and seeing were two different things. Death was an abstract tragedy. Seeing what they'd done to him—the hatred and disrespect poured into that display— "He deserved so much better." Better from the people Derian had spent his life trying to protect. Better from the knights who had failed him in the end.

From Ádan.

"You coming inside?" V asked as they passed through the Academy gate and put a wall between Ádan and any more visions the tree wanted to give him.

That had been Ádan's plan, but, "No. I need to—I'm going to —I have another errand to run."

Varajas wasn't fooled by Ádan's stumbling evasion. He put a hand on Ádan's shoulder. Wordless acceptance. "Tell Korin hi for me."

4

ÁDAN MOVED THROUGH the evening city like a shadow. He crept through alleys, over rooftops, muffling his already soft steps with magic and wrapping darkness around himself like a blanket.

He knew this city, knew its secret pathways and shortcuts. Knew its dangers as well as he knew its pleasures. A gift Derian had given Ádan, that after he'd joined the knights, Ádan spent more years here than in Ulek. Triome would never be exile to him. It was home.

How long had Derian known what was coming? How long had he been laying plans, preparing for this possibility? Fourteen years ago, when he'd sent Ádan to Ritalle under orders to make friends with Lysander, to worm his way into the Prince's confidence, had Derian been thinking about politics, or had he, even then, been creating a bolt-hole for Ádan to escape to when the world fell down around them?

It was full dark by the time Ádan reached the boarding house. Korin's shutters were open, and a warm light filled his window. Ádan climbed the building across the alley. From the roof, he had a clear view into Korin's room.

Korin was there, sitting on his bed, eyes closed. Meditating or doing magic—Ádan couldn't tell which. Either way, Ádan was in no rush to interrupt him. Just the sight of Korin eased something in Ádan he hadn't realized had been held tense.

When Ádan had left, Korin had still been recovering from his ordeal with the cultists. He looked so much better now. Relaxed, healthy.

Beautiful. After everything Ádan had seen in Ulek, it was a relief to find Korin safe. Not that Ádan had any reason to suspect otherwise, but still…

Derian's body hanging…

Ádan shoved that thought away.

Korin. Better to think about Korin. Ádan had missed him, worried about him, more than was warranted by the fact they'd only known each other a few weeks. Since Ádan had to ride south to meet Lysander, they'd been apart longer than they'd been together. How had Korin so quickly become so central to Ádan's thoughts? To his life?

Everything felt so fragile right now—the future, the world. Everything Ádan knew in his life had been shattered and he was still feeling his way through the aftermath. Given that, it was no surprise the hesitation, the fear that was keeping him here, lurking in shadows. The last time they'd talked, Korin was still recovering from almost getting killed. He was still working through the shock of finding out what Ádan was. Now, in Ádan's absence, Korin would have had time to think—what if he'd changed his mind about wanting to be with Ádan?

When they'd first met, Korin had needed Ádan's help. Ádan had been happy to offer it, especially once he'd realized the kind of wizard Korin was. What had started with Ádan cultivating Korin as an asset had turned into something more. Something bigger, that Ádan knew was dangerous.

The simple truth was the tables had turned. Right now, Ádan needed Korin. He needed someone alive and warm and safe. If

Korin had changed his mind while Ádan was away, had decided he didn't want to see Ádan...

Ádan stood. He took a running leap, using magic to give him the momentum he needed to land on Korin's roof and more magic to keep the impact silent. Reflex, rather than intent. He wasn't trying to sneak up. Ádan just hated making noise.

Korin opened his eyes as Ádan dropped through the open window and his face lit up with a wide, open smile that immediately burned away every one of Ádan's doubts. "Hi."

Ádan returned the smile reflexively. It was hard not to smile at Korin. "Hey, Sunshine."

Which left them grinning at each other like idiots. And that wouldn't do. So Ádan took the two steps necessary to reach Korin on the bed, hauled him up by his arms, and kissed him.

It was a relief. It was everything he'd been dreaming of: Korin, warm and solid against him. Alive. His pulse under Ádan's fingers, his breath hot on Ádan's cheek.

Korin pulled his head back, still smiling. "I saw you today, in the parade. I hoped that you'd..." his gaze dropped and he blushed, "well, this."

"And here I am." Light words, teasing tone. Korin deserved a happy reunion. Ádan's burdens were his own.

"Can you stay?"

The naked hope in Korin's soft blue eyes would have melted Ádan if Ádan weren't already utterly undone. "My night is yours."

Korin flushed a brighter red, and pulled Ádan with him back onto the bed.

Figuring people out—that was Ádan's job, and he was developing an in-depth mental file on Korin. He knew, for example, that Korin's embarrassment at that moment wasn't about sex. They'd only been together twice, but Korin had never shown a lack of comfort in his body—with the exception of his hands. Korin wasn't shy of the physical. Wasn't afraid to see or be seen.

No, it hadn't taken Ádan long to figure out that what embarrassed Korin was the wanting itself. Korin felt bad for thinking of himself, for admitting his own desires—be they for a sugary treat or for a night of being ravished. Ádan didn't know who to blame for that—whether it was a mindset instilled by Korin's teacher Teriad and his rather obvious desire to be a martyr, or whether it came from former lover Jonathan, who had used Korin carelessly, based on every story Korin had told.

It didn't matter. Ádan was here now and Ádan was happy to give Korin whatever Korin wanted.

Ádan ignored the flare of guilt. He was good at that. He didn't need to listen to the little voice saying how convenient it was that his generosity towards Korin would also go a long way toward pushing the waking nightmares out of Ádan's mind.

Certainly, giving Korin what he wanted was no hardship. Ádan relished the solid warmth of Korin's skin as he slid his hands beneath Korin's shirt. Ádan watched Korin's face, the little tensions and relaxations that played across it as Ádan explored Korin's body. Like learning to play an instrument.

And Korin was the best kind of instrument—the sort that wanted to play Ádan right back. Korin knew—Light above, did Korin know—how to find Ádan's sensitive spots. Where to brush by and where to linger and—

Ádan caught Korin's hands as Korin worked them under the waistband of Ádan's pants. Korin's still-gloved hands. Ádan wanted Korin, not the rough, prickly linen. Korin tensed—not in the good way. Nervous of attention paid, nervous, in this one small way, of being seen.

Ádan slid his fingers under the gloves. He circled his thumbs over Korin's palms, felt Korin squirm beneath him. The skin was rough, textured. Ádan was learning the map of Korin's scars, the lines and ripples that ran over his palms and up Korin's fingers.

Korin let out a tiny whimper as Ádan lifted Korin's hands, peeled the gloves back, and traced the same path with his tongue. This was the truth that only Ádan knew. Korin might hide these hands away, but he loved the attention Ádan gave them. This was all it took to melt Korin, to open him up, to make him desperate for more.

Korin, tonight, seemed determined to give as well as he got. He leaned in, pressed his cheek to Ádan's, and let out a long, warm breath against Ádan's ear. Followed by his tongue tracing a teasing path along the outside edge.

Ádan moaned. He couldn't help himself. And any thoughts of long, leisurely foreplay evaporated. "Clothes—off." He'd meant that to sound like an order, but Korin's tongue made him shiver and it came out more of a plea.

Korin obeyed all the same, biting his lip over a pleased-with-himself smile as he hurried to undress. Ádan squirmed out of his own clothes, his eyes never leaving Korin.

Naked, Korin pushed Ádan back on Korin's narrow bed and bent down to take Ádan into his mouth. Ádan groaned at the wet heat, at Korin's swirling tongue. In this, too, Korin knew what he was about.

It wasn't enough. Ádan slid his fingers through Korin's hair and applied enough pressure to be clear he didn't want Korin to stop as he twisted around, got himself turned in the other direction, and slid his head between Korin's kneeling legs.

Ádan wrapped his arms around Korin's thighs, closed his eyes, gave himself over entirely to sheer physical sensation. To Korin's cock filling his mouth, to the slick, sweaty heat of Korin's body along his, to the blissful touch of Korin's lips and tongue. It drove away everything else.

So easy to lose himself in the pleasure of it. Until his pleasure crested. Until Korin, too, came with a gasp and a sigh. He rolled off Ádan then stretched out next to him, one arm draped across Ádan's stomach. With a sated, heavy-lidded smile, he said, "Welcome home."

$\mathcal{K}$ORIN CURLED IN, rested his head on Ádan's shoulder. The sheer decadence of lying in a bed with his lover—Korin wasn't going to get tired of that any time soon. "How was your trip?"

With his hand on Ádan's chest, Korin could feel Ádan's heartbeat speed up. "Nothing I need to repeat any time soon," Ádan said. An answer and a non-answer. A clear hint he didn't want to talk about it.

Which Korin could respect. There were things he wasn't ready to talk about either. "Now that you're back..." Korin paused, unsure what he wanted to say. Or ask. Or even what he was allowed.

Ádan lay his own hand over Korin's, laced their fingers together. But he didn't say anything.

They'd left things up in the air. Part of that was because Korin had still been recovering when Ádan had been summoned by Prince Lysander. He hadn't been in any shape to make real decisions. But the rest was the sheer enormity of the things they had yet to talk about.

Ádan was a wizard-knight, had lied to Korin about who he was and why he'd approached Korin in the first place. Ádan was trying to carry on the work of his order, was tied inextricably to the tree.

The tree, the tree—that haunted Korin's dreams, that spoke through his nightmares. Korin wanted nothing to do with the tree, with the knights, with Ádan's cause.

He just wanted Ádan.

Which was probably a sign of terrible judgement. Ádan had deceived him. Ádan had drawn Korin into this business without warning him of the cost. Ádan had needed help and he'd used Korin to get that help.

But on the other hand, Ádan was kind. Ádan listened. Ádan *saw* Korin.

Ádan had saved Korin's life.

"Tell me about your day," Ádan murmured, his breath warm in Korin's hair.

"It wasn't anything exciting. I healed people."

"I like hearing you talk about that."

So Korin talked about the colds, the bad backs, the little girl with her broken arm. Ádan listened, smiling at some of Korin's descriptions, asking questions whenever Korin paused. Before, when they'd talked like this, Korin hadn't known the truth about Ádan. It was different now, knowing that Ádan understood magic —even if he wasn't versed in Korin's specific magic—because Korin could really talk about observations, thoughts, theories, and Ádan understood enough to at least nod along.

Korin couldn't deny how nice it was to have someone to talk to.

And when he reached the point where he was yawning more than he was making words, Ádan pulled the sheet up over them both. It was too sticky-hot to sleep pressed against each other, but Ádan rested his hand on Korin's hip and dropped a kiss on Korin's shoulder. "Sleep well, Sunshine."

· · ·

THE NEXT MORNING, Ádan was gone. The girls in the kitchen teased Korin for the smile he wore when he came down for a bowl of sweet rice porridge. They asked if he'd been dreaming of someone, giggled when he blushed. It felt nice to be seen, to be known. In return, he asked Verania about her cousin, who had just earned a scholarship to the school of the Balance, and Holli about the bird sketches that were her latest hobby. That was nice too, knowing. This family he got to be part of day after day.

Korin brought a glass of pineapple juice in with him to the bar, getting ready to start his work. He settled in, still thinking about Ádan as he waited for the day's first patient to show up. He didn't have to wait long.

Korin recognized the man as soon as he limped into Marta's guesthouse, supported on one side by the teenage niece who had hugged Korin the last time he'd fixed her uncle. The man had had a broken leg—an old injury that had healed on its own, but so badly set so it had twisted his leg to near uselessness. Korin had fixed that. Which was why it made no sense the man was limping again.

Another broken leg would have been unusual, but not impossible. As the girl eased the man into a chair, it looked like his leg had been broken again, set wrong again, then healed back into the exact same twist. Which wasn't possible.

On top of that, both man and niece were avoiding Korin's eyes, leaning away, their every body language expressing fear and discomfort. As though Korin had never helped them before.

"Jere, right?" Korin asked, addressing the man.

The man nodded without meeting Korin's eyes. The niece, whose name Korin couldn't remember, said, "You need to fix him for real this time." Fear didn't keep the anger out of her voice.

"I don't understand," Korin admitted.

"It wore off!" Now she looked at Korin, challenging. "What you did stopped working!"

Which left Korin even more confused. "Magic doesn't work

like that. It doesn't wear off. Once I fix something, it's just fixed. It can't—"

It couldn't do exactly what Korin saw in front of him. "I'm sorry." Korin took a breath, lowered his voice back to a soothing tone. "Obviously it has. If you'll let me, I can put it right."

To get a real sense of what was happening, Korin needed direct contact. He peeled off his gloves and tried to ignore how Jere flinched away from Korin's ragged skin. He rolled up Jere's loose trousers to expose the leg. It looked exactly the same as it had before. When Korin reached in with magic, it felt exactly the same as it had before. Korin could find no trace of evidence that he had ever healed it.

So he healed it again. And if Jere was less profligate in his thanks than before, Korin could hardly blame him.

After they left, Korin ducked back into the kitchen. "I need to go out," he said to Verania. "Apologize to anyone who comes looking for me. If it's someone in urgent need, find out their address and I'll go to them."

Korin had someone he needed to talk to.

RENÉE WAS TEACHING THIS MORNING, which meant Korin had to brave the crowds at the school of the Balance to find her. A sprawling campus in the heart of the city, the school occupied more land than the entire village in which Korin had been born. Dormitories, classroom buildings, parks, arenas—so much space— and at the center, at the heart of everything, the tower.

Korin had been making use of the library almost since he arrived, and by now the the gate guards knew him and waved him through. When he asked after Renée, the guard pointed across the lush green lawn so different from anything Korin had ever known and to the tower itself.

Impossibly tall, constructed of a dusky pink marble that turned translucent in the morning sun, the tower of the Balance was a wonder. Like so many buildings in the city, it was topped with a golden dome, this one polished so bright Korin had to shield his eyes to look at it. It was the tallest building in the city, despite the fact that the tower's base was in the valley and the palace had been built on the cliffs that stood high over the river.

There was another set of guards at the tower doors. At the Crystal—Korin's school—there had been zero guards. But that school had been isolated and inaccessible, on the most frozen tip of the most frozen country in the world. No one came to the Crystal unless they had business there.

The Balance was a wizard school, like all the rest, but non-wizards came here too. Most of the nobility sent their children to be educated here. Craftspeople gave demonstrations. For anyone in the nation of Ritalle who wanted something beyond a basic education, this was the place to be. Which meant keeping a close eye on who came and who went.

Korin was a wizard. No one questioned his right to be here—even if his Staff sigil earned him some dark looks. Korin climbed the great winding staircase as fast as he could until he found the classroom where Renée was teaching. He slipped in and took a seat in the back, behind the sea of children Renée was lecturing.

There might have been more students in this one class than had been in the entire school of the Crystal. Renée lectured about magnetism, moving between notes on the chalkboard and an array of magnets on the table at the front of the room where she illuminated and manipulated the magnetic fields with a wave of her hand. It was enough of a show she had the room's full attention. It helped that she seemed to be having an incredibly good time.

This was magic: making ten-to-twelve-year-olds laugh as the laws of physics danced before their eyes. And Korin laughed along with them as Renée waggled her eyebrows and faked surprise and generally held the room spellbound.

When Renée released the class, Korin stayed in his seat as the hoard of laughing children trampled past. Once he could see the front of the room again, Renée was smiling at him. "I thought I saw you sneak in."

"I was in the neighborhood."

"Uh huh." She tilted her head, smile falling away. "What's got you looking serious?"

Was it so obvious? "I have a magic question for you."

"Oh this should be good." She started gathering up magnets, warping the fields around them so they'd all fit together in the box, manipulating the energy with the same casual ease as Korin had when he healed bodies. "Lay it on me."

She was treating this lightly, but that was Renée. "Can magic just undo itself? Stop working and revert to the way it was?"

Renée fit the last magnet into the box, closed the lid, and set it on the table. She hopped herself up to sit next to it, her feet swinging casually beneath. "You mean like an enchantment?"

"No, I mean if I heal someone and later they come back and what I did just...went away. Like I never worked the magic in the first place."

"That isn't possible," she said with confidence.

"That's what I thought. Except this morning someone came in and that's exactly what happened."

She tapped at her chin, thoughtful. "Do you mean you saw it happen? You saw the magic flip? Or they came back and they were back the way they had been?"

Korin didn't understand why it mattered. "The second one. But isn't that basically the same thing?"

"The difference, my dear boy, is all the difference. You're telling me your patients returned and were un-healed, and couldn't tell you how or why?"

"Yes. They said the magic undid itself. And I saw the injury. This wasn't that he'd somehow hurt himself again in the exact same way. It was as if my magic had never happened."

Renée nodded, feet still swinging. "As if."

His magic *had* happened. "I healed him before. I know I did."

"Exactly. Well. There is one explanation that pops quite readily to my mind, being the suspicious old woman that I am."

She paused, giving Korin a chance to think it through, but he shook his head. "I don't see it."

"Of course you don't, because it's horrific. But it's the reversing itself that's the clue. Reversed, yes, but not by itself. Korin, some other wizard is going around undoing your work."

Korin opened his mouth to protest, but his mind spun through the arguments before he could get the words out. It wasn't possible. Except, of course it was. The exact same process he used to heal—someone could step back the change, take the body back the same way Korin did. But they couldn't, because that would be monstrous. Except…Korin knew perfectly well that there were monsters.

So instead of saying *no*, Korin asked, "Who would do that?"

"Someone who doesn't like what you're doing."

"I'm healing people. Who could have a problem with that?"

Renée shook her head and said nothing.

6

*Á*DAN ADDED ANOTHER book to the growing pile he'd started in what had once been some officer's private study. He'd chosen this room because it already had shelves of records lining the walls, and now he was working his way through the rest of the safehouse to find any other writings—histories, journals, even accounting ledgers—that might give him some new insight of how to move forward.

As he turned to resume his search, he saw Nikki and V at the door, blocking his exit. "Ádan," V began. "We need to talk."

"I know." Ádan was happy to talk. Eager, even. The trouble was, he knew what questions they were going to ask and damned if he had any answers for them. "Can it wait till I'm done with this?"

Nikki eyed the teetering tower Ádan was building. "What are you even doing?"

"Research."

There was silence as they waited for him to say more. Ádan offered nothing else. Finally, V said, "You know, if you told us what you were looking for, we might be able to help."

"If I knew what I was looking for, I'd tell you."

"That's bullshit." Nikki crossed his arms, his ice-blue eyes narrow with judgement. "You know something, and you're not telling us."

Varajas added, "There are only three of us left."

"You think I haven't noticed that?" Ádan snapped in response.

Varajas continued, his voice patient. "All I'm saying is we need to work as a team. Together."

Ádan matched his tone. Two could play the cool and collected game. "And all I'm saying is I'm trying to figure out how we do that. How three of us do the work of an entire order. How we protect the knife. How we protect ourselves. I can't tell you how that's going to work, and until I can…"

"Oh for fuck's sake." Nikki slapped the door in frustration. "Who said you had to figure it out by yourself? Let us *help.*"

"I appreciate the offer." But Grandmaster Derian had handed this responsibility to Ádan when he'd placed the knife in his hands. If they succeeded—if they failed—it was on Ádan's shoulders. As it had been on Derian's, on his predecessor's, stretching all the way back to Grandmaster Alín who had first taken on this burden.

On the other hand, Ádan understood just how hard it was to stand around and wait for orders, feeling like you should be doing *something.* "Okay. If you want to help, the first step is to tear this safehouse apart, and pick through any stone still standing in the Academy. If there are records to be found, I want to find them. Any writing down to some squire's grocery list. We've lost so much knowledge, we can't afford to lose any more."

"We can do that," Varajas said evenly. "And after?"

"After will depend on what we find. On if we end up knowing any more than we do now."

Which wasn't much. Ádan wasn't sure V and Nikki realized just how little they knew. How thin were the threads at which Ádan was grasping.

That had been one of the most frightening parts of that last night before Ádan, Nikhil, and Varajas had fled Ulek. Derian had talked to Ádan, had made a final confession, knowing it would be the last time they would talk in this world.

They'd been together in Derian's bedroom—one of the few parts of the castle where the wards still held well enough they could trust no wizard might be spying on them. The knife lay on the bed, its rippling blade pulsing with malice. Derian had held himself rigidly, like he was having to fight to keep from reaching for it.

"She can't be destroyed. That's the awful truth." Derian's hand twitched before he caught himself and crossed his arms. His handsome, firstborn face had aged terribly just in the last few months, drawn and hollow from too much magic and too little sleep. "We've had some of the best theorists who ever lived study her, and they've tried to find a weakness, but it just isn't possible. Something about the knife—something we don't understand." His hands closed to fists. "What *do* we understand? Nothing. Even after all these years…"

He'd trailed off, taken a deep breath, found his focus again. "Maybe they knew more—Alín and Tiarna, when they first took on this burden. Maybe we've lost information over the years. Maybe we never had it. If that knowledge does exist, it's buried somewhere, lost in some corner no one has looked for a very long time.

"What I do know is that she'll whisper to you. She'll creep into your dreams. She'll try to get you to use her, to set her free. There's no way to stop that. But you can't. We can't. If her power were set free, it could be the end of everything. The death of…"

He fell silent again, his eyes growing unfocused. He wasn't looking at Ádan anymore. "She lies," he whispered. "She lies. You have to remember. Above all else. She lies."

The emptiness in his voice had been terrifying. Whatever nightmare he'd been living, it had been worse than Ádan had known. The full burden, the responsibility he had passed to Ádan was enormous. Even now, Ádan was only beginning to grasp the whole of it. Was Ádan going to become that haunted, hollow man?

When he let himself slow down long enough to think, he knew he had taken the first step down that path. A path lined with the creaking sound of a body hanging from a rope, a shadow that would follow Ádan forever.

The other fear, equally terrible, was that whatever connection previous Grandmasters had with the knife—some step or ritual Ádan hadn't been able to fulfill—Ádan would never have. What if Ádan never heard its voice? *Her* voice. And that became the failure that would ruin what tenuous future the knights still had.

Ádan could share none of these fears with his friends. Derian had chosen him to be the leader. He couldn't begin that duty by undermining whatever faith they had in him. After everything that had happened, if they knew just how lost he truly was, it could all fall apart.

Varajas, who had been looking around the office, seemingly unaware of the struggle going on inside Ádan's head, said, "If nothing else, this gives me something to do. I won't be leaving the house for a while."

That jerked Ádan's focus back to the here and now. "Why not?"

A thin, cynical smile. "When you rode back with Lysander, did you not notice the rest of the people riding with you?"

"Darkivels," Ádan said with poison. "But they don't know you. They shouldn't."

"Not them. High Father Donatien and his blades. I saw a number of familiar faces. Including Ruan."

Most people had history before they joined the knights. Ádan had been recruited young, but that wasn't true of everyone. The rule was, your past didn't matter. Whoever or whatever you had been before you joined didn't matter. Your oaths started you fresh. Ádan didn't know the details of Varajas's history, other than that,

somehow, he'd run afoul of the blades. That one in particular—
Brother Ruan—had hunted him for years.

Blades were the arm of the church that hunted wizards who
had broken the rules. Since the knights had started—all those
hundreds and hundreds of years ago—with a wizard who had
turned his back on the laws and the orders, the blades had been
suspicious of them from the start. High Father Donatien had been
quick to side with the Darkivels when they'd first made noise
about moving against the knights.

Blades in the city weren't much of a threat to Ádan. His cover
was solid. Nikki, similarly, had been kept away from the front lines
by Derian, so he'd be safe to move around. But Varajas was right.
He'd have to stay hidden until the High Father turned his eye to
some new project.

One more thing for Ádan to worry about. He didn't want
anything bad to happen to his friend, of course. He cared about V.
But also, they simply couldn't afford to lose another knight.

So many things to keep track of. So many things to think
about. How had Derian done this? And he'd had the whole order
to run.

"All right then." Ádan was an expert at faking confidence.
"We're going to dig through the safehouse and the Academy. We're
going to find everything there is to find. And then we're going to
figure out how to move forward."

That seemed to satisfy Nikki and V. They nodded like he'd
given them an order, then left him alone again. Silence descended,
surrounded him, covered him like a blanket. Silence in which
Ádan strained to hear the barest whisper, the slightest breath, of
the object over which he now stood guardian.

More things he didn't know—whether or not he even needed
to be able to talk to it. But Derian had talked to it; he'd implied
that all previous guardians had been able to talk to it. That it was
good to know what the knife was thinking.

She lies. She lies.
Or maybe silence wasn't the worst thing after all.

7

*K*ORIN SAT IN his room, studying several new anatomy pamphlets he'd found at the Balance's library. There was nothing particularly ground-breaking, but the illustrations were beautifully done, and it was never a bad idea to refresh and remind himself how everything fit together.

He was focused in, tracing the lines of the nervous system with his finger, so it took him some time to notice the sound at his window.

Korin had closed the shutters this morning when a sudden rainstorm had blown up, and he hadn't gotten around to opening them back up now the sun was out. The wood of the shutters was thick—they did a fair job of blocking out noise from the alley—but this sounded like someone was standing outside his second story window and tapping on it with a hammer.

Or throwing rocks. Like Ádan had been known to do.

Korin jumped up. Threw open the shutters…

And startled a little green bird that fluttered away into the sky.

With a sigh, Korin returned to his work, leaving the shutters open.

The bird returned. It was a tiny thing, no bigger than Korin's hand. It flew in the open window, shimmering emerald feathers gleaming in the sunlight. It landed on the little table Korin used as a desk.

Korin shooed it away with his hand. The bird fluttered up to the ceiling, then landed back on the table.

This was not a problem Korin had in the south. Probably because it was usually too cold there for open windows.

Waving his arms wildly, Korin managed to chase the bird back out of his room. He closed the shutters again. He'd miss the breeze, but until the wildlife had decided to move on, better to just lock it out.

This time, when the tapping started back up, it was a multi-part harmony of light and heavy, fast and slow. Like a whole flock had gathered outside Korin's window. Korin peeked through the crack at the shutter's edge and, yes, there it was. A wild fluttering hurricane of feathers.

This was no accident of nature. This was magic.

He needed to see what was going on. Rather than open his window again and risk a whole flock in his room, Korin went outside.

As soon as Korin stepped into the alley, the flock dove out of the sky and surrounded him. Korin froze in the cloud of fluttering birds the color of jewels. Wings batted against him, claws and beaks scraped dangerously close to his skin. He coughed against the overwhelming musty smell of feathers. What in the Prophet's name *was* this?

The little green bird that had started it all landed on Korin's shoulder and in a quick, sharp motion pecked against his cheek. It stung, but didn't draw blood. "You have my attention," Korin said, unsure what else to do.

The flock lifted into the air. Moving as one, it set off down the street, drawing pointing hands and exclamations of delight from people it passed.

Korin watched it go, and after a few seconds, the little green bird—which was still on his shoulder—pecked him again. Harder this time.

"Am I supposed to follow?" There was no response. Korin wasn't sure what he had expected. But when he set off down the street in the direction the rest of the birds had gone, he didn't get pecked again.

The birds led Korin through the city, away from the harbor, towards the bluffs that housed the wealthiest nobles in Triome—possibly in the whole of Ritalle. Korin had been up there once, had sat in a little park with Ádan and looked out across the beautiful city. Light only knew what waited for him this time.

Magic—this had to be magic, and enchanted flocks of birds were pretty much a tool employed by wizards of only one order. There was plenty of overlap in magic techniques among the nine orders, but only one order taught its wizards to work with animals of any sort—the Order of the Wing.

Korin crossed the river and followed the birds up the steep walking paths that led to the top of the cliffs. What sort of wizard was going to be waiting for Korin at the top? Someone pissed off because Korin had been offering for free the healing services the local wing wizards made fortunes off of? That was the only thing Korin could imagine. Why else would one of them have any interest in Korin? Enough interest to use this dramatically elaborate spell to draw him?

At the top of the cliff, Korin stopped again as he saw the road the flock now hovered over. It took another peck at his neck to get him moving again.

The birds were taking him to the royal palace.

ANOTHER PECK from the green bird, and this time Korin felt a drop of blood ooze from the spot. Which took only the barest thought to heal, but the message was clear. Keep going. Keep going towards the palace.

How was he going to get in? Were the sentries going to let a wizard in shabby clothes through because he was escorted by a flock of birds? The thought was absurd.

And wrong. Just outside the main gate, Korin spotted a young man dressed in elegant black, an elaborately jeweled wing sigil in plain view around his neck. The man held a staff taller than him, with a hooked top. From the hook at the top, a furry creature of reddish brown hung upside down, its small black eyes locked on Korin. A bat, it had to be, except that he had never seen one so big. The creature was bigger than Korin's head. Wizard and bat watched Korin approach.

As Korin got close, the man gave a graceful, sweeping bow. The staff in his hand never wavered. "Welcome, Korin of the Staff. I am Samir of the Wing. I was sent to wait for you and escort you to her Ladyship, the Archwizard Sheluna zhi Darkivel."

"Excuse me?" Korin asked, surprised. He couldn't imagine being of interest to any Archwizard—particularly to Sheluna.

The bat—Samir's familiar?—chittered. Samir absently reached over with his free hand and scratched the top of its head. "Please come with me. Archwizard Sheluna can answer your questions better than I." Samir flicked a finger toward the bird on Korin's shoulder and it flew off. "Please," he repeated. "It isn't good to keep her waiting."

What else could Korin do?

Korin was consumed with curiosity. About why he was here. About the palace they walked through. And about Samir himself, who was so unlike other wizards Korin had known.

Wing wizards were almost universally attractive. When a person spent their life immersed in magics of the body, that magic changed you. Any wizard of the Staff or the Wing ended up becoming the person they imagined themself to be. But with the Wing, there always seemed to be an extra layer of gloss, and Samir had taken that to an extreme. It went without saying he was gorgeous. A perfect smile on a perfect face. Toned brown skin that almost glowed with the warmth of health, layered over sculpted muscles. Soft and shining black hair that hung to his shoulders with ends just starting to curl. He looked more like a work of art than a living, breathing person. Beautiful, but in a way that made him seem removed, untouchable. A statue that had come to life.

Korin dragged his attention away from the man at his side to take in the palace itself. It was huge and sprawling, a collection of buildings of various heights tied together with elegant arching walkways and covered paths. All the space in between was filled with bright, fragrant gardens.

Not guards, not anyone questioned Samir and Korin as they wandered through the royal spaces. Finally, they reached a circular building set apart from the rest, with its own ring of domed towers around the edge of its roof and an open courtyard at the center, with greenery everywhere. Samir led them up the curving staircase attached to the outer wall, to the garden above.

The garden was lush and thick, with walkways leading between broad-leaved greenery and bright, oversized flowers. Voices filtered through the garden—talking, laughing. And other sounds. Animal sounds. A screech. A cry. A growl. As the sea breeze stirred branches and stems, Korin caught sight of the people on the roof as they lounged in or walked through the garden. Mostly elegant wizards in black. Wing wizards, with a menagerie of familiars. No question about it—Korin did not belong here.

The order of the Wing had been the first of the wizard orders. Its founder had created the whole system. That creator—the very first Archwizard—had been a Darkivel. Since then, while the other orders had expanded and evolved over time, the order of the Wing had always been led by a Darkivel. The leadership passed down like clockwork, always grandparent to grandchild, with one gifted child born every other generation.

In combination with the strange red eyes that marked every gifted Darkivel child, along with the credible rumors of the family's dealings with demons and outsiders—not to mention the brutal deaths the family's enemies tended to suffer—suffice to say, the Darkivels had a reputation. They were heroes now, but that was more a testament to the hatred the world had turned on Ulek and the knights than any noble quality the Darkivel's had demonstrated.

And now Sheluna zhi Darkivel wanted to see Korin.

Samir waved Korin forward. No guards at the door, no servants to announce Korin's presence. Why should there be? No one would dare to intrude on Archwizard Sheluna's sanctuary without an invitation. Even with an invitation, Korin had to steel himself to continue.

In Ulek, Korin had met plenty of Wing wizards. To the last, they'd been haughty, self-involved, and over-impressed with their own abilities. Darkivel Archwizards had a long history of flaunting their power, their untouchable position, to play fast and loose with the laws their own ancestor had created. The rest of the Wing order took their cues from there. As a wizard of another order, Korin should have been no business of Sheluna's. She had no authority over him. No right to summon him. No reason to take any interest in him at all.

As Korin passed into the shade, a cool wave of air passed over him and made him shiver. For the first time since he'd arrived in Triome, Korin wasn't dressed warm enough. It was magic, of course, cooling the rooftop to an environment comfortable for southern wizards in their dark, heavy clothes. It reminded Korin of the lands he'd left behind. The lands he didn't miss.

Korin crossed the roof, and the voices around him dropped to whispers.

On the far side, the trees and bushes opened up on a mosaicked circle with a fountain in the center and a ring of couches and benches. A dozen wizards sat in comfortable arrangement. Cats and dogs and lizards and birds darted about in a chaos that defied counting.

At the center of everything, Archwizard Sheluna. She reclined on a pile of cushions arranged on one of the couches, her silver-blonde hair loose across her shoulders and her red eyes glowing. She wore a flowing dress of black velvet, embroidered in blue and gold with the sigils of the Wing and the Darkivel crest. Too heavy for Triome's weather. Flaunting the fact she didn't have to care.

As Korin stepped into the open area, Sheluna looked over at him, a sweet smile spreading across her lovely face. "Oh, finally. Our guest has arrived."

Soft pressure against the small of Korin's back. He turned to look, and froze.

A tiger, its head level with Korin's chest, stared back.

---

8

*Á*DAN LURKED IN the hall outside the entrance to the royal archives. A clerk sat at the desk beside the door, keeping guard. Technically, Ádan wasn't allowed in the archives. In a pinch, if he got caught, he could say Lysander sent him, and the prince would back him up. But it would draw attention. Ádan didn't want attention. Therefore, best if he didn't get caught.

Fortunately, this was the magic Ádan was best at. This was what he'd been trained in from the start.

It took barely a thought to draw whispers and shadows close, making himself dim. Not invisible, but hard to see, hard to focus on. Eyes and minds would slip past him without catching.

Another twitch of power summoned a rustling noise that drew the clerk's attention as Ádan slid by him. He opened the archive doors quickly, but quietly, and eased them closed again without making a sound.

Inside, he listened. He'd checked around, charming his way through people to make sure no one would be using the archives at this time, but there was no reason to be sloppy. He counted his breaths, eyes closed, and only when he'd reached sixty without even the tiniest scratch of movement around him did he relax.

This wasn't the first time Ádan had broken into the archives, so he knew his way around, knew exactly what section he needed. Still moving noiselessly, he wound his way through the labyrinthine stacks to the shelves that would hold the history he sought.

This was recent history, as the Kingdom of Ritalle measured things. A little over a hundred years ago. Just before the Knights had been banished from the city. At that time, Lysander's father had still been alive. Had still been king. Lysander's father the king had a younger brother—the man who would have been Lysander's uncle, had he lived to see Lysander born.

The brother hadn't lived. In fact, his death had been what sparked the final explosion between the royal family and the Knights that had culminated in the Knights being driven from Triome.

Ádan had heard this story from Derian, and then again from Lysander. At the time, it had been clear the death had been somehow tied to the knife. Now, Ádan needed details—specific details. He had a suspicion he needed confirmed.

It didn't take much digging before Ádan found the notes from the wizards who had treated the sick prince. Ádan read through them several times, memorizing key details. *Loose skin. Lines of rot. Reacts badly to magic.*

The notes documented a progressive sense of frustration and helplessness. From the tight, careful script of the first wizard who had looked at the prince—a Wing wizard who taught at the school —to the urgent scrawl of the Archwizard of the Wing himself who had been called in when the prince's condition had continued to deteriorate.

That had been Sheluna's grandfather, her predecessor in leadership of the order. Reading his words now, the anger that simmered behind them as this powerful man faced something he couldn't understand—Ádan wondered how many seeds of the war that had erupted almost a hundred years later had been planted here.

It hardly mattered. The past was just that. The important thing was, as far as Ádan could tell, the prince had died of the blight.

Ádan carefully returned the documents to the shelf, replacing them exactly as they'd been before. Then he slipped out, as quietly as he'd come in.

The blight. Which Ádan had never seen or heard of before a month ago, when he'd first met Korin and Korin had led him to that sick old man.

Ádan still felt bad about how he'd lied to Korin, but he'd been desperate. He was still desperate, and the world was only getting more complicated.

Ádan had seen knights afflicted in similar ways to the blight. At the end of the war, when loss had started to look inevitable, Derian had been willing to try anything, including letting the remaining knights open themselves to the influence they were supposed to be guarding against. They'd taken in the knife's power.

It hadn't saved them.

Then, here in Triome, Ádan had seen more of that in the blight. At first, he'd been terrified it meant the knife's power had somehow gotten free. That he'd already failed as a guardian.

In that case, it had turned out to be something else. Once again, people who had opened themselves up to the influence of the knife. People who shouldn't have been able to, mind you. But still, an intentional use of the power.

Now, reading about the dead prince, Ádan had questions again. Questions about the true limitations of the knife. Questions about the protections that might not be as secure as everyone believed. Or, conversely, had the prince known about it? Had he done this to himself? Had someone else done it to him? Who? And why?

So much he didn't know; so many things he was—let's be honest—going to need help understanding. It was overwhelming to think about.

But he couldn't let that show. Walking through the palace, he had to be Ádan zhi Dhari, who didn't have a thought in his head beyond clothes and parties and wild adventures with the prince. Ádan forced a smile, put more energy into his walk. Became the empty-headed libertine the court expected to see, a man without a single care.

No one would have any idea that he was wrestling with questions of how to stop a threat to the very world.

KORIN STOOD eye-to-eye with the tiger, unsure what to do next. Until Sheluna said, "That's right, Cír. Bring him to me."

The tiger—Cír—Sheluna's familiar, took Korin's arm in his mouth. Teeth as long as Korin's fingers pressed into Korin's skin. Not quite painful. Absolutely terrifying. Cír tugged, and Korin went along as the tiger pulled Korin towards Sheluna.

Korin pulsed magic to keep his breathing even and his heartbeat calm. It wouldn't do to show fear to either of the two predators watching him. Cír released Korin and circled behind Sheluna, moving with a silence that shouldn't have been possible for something of its bulk.

Sheluna smiled and lay a graceful hand on her tiger's flank, but her strange red eyes never left Korin. "So you're the boy my wizards are making such a fuss about."

Korin wasn't sure how to answer that, so he stayed quiet. Around and behind him, the whispers continued, but Korin didn't dare let his attention stray from Sheluna. All her beauty and relaxed air couldn't hide the fact that she was as much a danger as the familiar that paced back and forth behind her.

"Staff wizards." Sheluna sighed. "Always so uptight. At least, the ones of you who are worth anything. You can relax, Korin. I didn't invite you here to feed you to the tiger." She stood, her movements as graceful as the giant cat at her side. "I have other plans. Better plans. Walk with me."

Curious despite himself, Korin followed.

Sheluna led Korin away from the building full of wizards and out into one of the central gardens. Cír paced in a wide circle around them as they walked, and whether it was Sheluna herself or the tiger—or both—no one else approached. Their conversation was private.

"Why did you send those birds after me?" Korin asked as they moved onto a crushed-shells path that cut through a long line of roses.

"I wanted to meet you," Sheluna said, as though the answer were obvious.

Korin was feeling brave enough to say, "Seems a bit dramatic."

"It was a summoning spell." Sheluna shrugged her perfect shoulders. "What did *your* teachers do if they needed to see you?"

"They sent a note."

Sheluna's red eyes glowed—literally—with amusement. "How pedestrian. And which school was that, where wizards were afraid to use magic?"

Korin managed to keep any defensiveness out of his voice. "The crystal."

"I see. You're from Torar, then? Grew up in the south? How ever did you manage to end up here?"

Was she making fun of him? She was so dry, Korin couldn't tell. Why would she care about the details of Korin's history? Korin was no one and she was the Archwizard zhi Darkivel.

Korin answered honestly, if carefully. "After I earned my sigil, I traveled. My master—Teriad—he took us around healing people. We ended up in Ulek, healing soldiers and wizards who needed it. Until the war ended, and I came here."

Ulek, the war, the Wizard-Knights had all followed him here. But that was the last thing he needed to be thinking about with Sheluna walking beside him.

Sheluna paused to lean over a powder-blue rose. "They have such lovely flowers here. I do love Ritalle for that." She sniffed it, smiled, continued walking.

Korin still wasn't sure what to think. Sheluna wasn't the first archwizard he'd met, but Perrault had been different. The Crystal, as an order, was the complete opposite of everything the Wing seemed to be. Perrault was, in so many ways, just another wizard, in an order full of people who cared almost nothing for what the world thought of him.

So far, Sheluna had shown Korin nothing but a carefully constructed facade. Whatever game she was playing, he was tired of it. "Why did you bring me here?"

A hint of a smile, like she was pleased with his directness. "You've been healing people."

Korin stopped walking. Now he understood what this was about. "There isn't a single person I've helped who could have afforded to go to one of your wizards."

"No, I would imagine not." Sheluna turned to face him, just as Cír stepped up to her side. She idly stroked his head as she talked. "It is curious, though. You have a gift—a skill. Something you've worked and studied for. Your time and talent are worth something, don't you think?"

"And it's my choice what I do with them."

"But why?" Sheluna pressed. "You can't help everyone who needs it. Surely you know that. Why exhaust yourself and possibly endanger yourself to make life better for a mere handful? In the grand scheme of things, how will those few lives you save even matter?"

That was exactly the sort of argument Korin expected from a wizard of the Wing. "People's lives matter to them. And who am I to say who does and doesn't matter?"

"Who indeed?" Sheluna smiled and her eyes pulsed. "Who you may be, my dear, is exactly what I'm looking for."

9

A LITTLE BENCH was tucked among the roses. Sheluna sat and waved for Korin to join her. It felt isolated, private. Especially with Cír prowling about beyond the bushes to make certain no one came too close. They wouldn't be disturbed, but Korin was sharply aware of how vulnerable he was. If Sheluna didn't like something he said, what would she do?

He didn't sit.

She gave a tilt of her head, acknowledging his choice. "You were there, in the war."

Korin nodded, although Sheluna's words hadn't been a question.

"You saw what happened. What it looks like when wizards make war against each other."

"Knights," Korin corrected. "We were fighting the knights."

"Semantics. What I'm talking about is warfare fought with magic, when both sides have it."

The knights had more than just magic. The knights had used the power of the tree, which was its own flavor of horror. But it still fit the point Sheluna seemed to be making, so Korin nodded.

Sheluna leaned forward, elbows on her knees. A strangely

casual position for an Archwizard. "The war in Ulek was years in the making. Father and I, we saw it coming. Talked to the church, to the King of Aleton and the Queen of Ritalle. I brought in the Archwizards of the Sword and the Flame and, eventually, the Balance. Thirty years of politics that led to ten years of fighting."

Forty years total. Almost twice as long as Korin had been alive.

"It was an immense effort; it required all our resources and attention. And now that it's over, a number of us are looking around at the world and not happy with what's happened while our focus was on Ulek. Power has shifted. People have been up to things while our backs were turned. But the last thing anyone wants right now is another war. Wouldn't you agree?"

"I can't speak for everyone, but I certainly don't want any more war." Although something in the way she was talking made it sound like a trick question. Like she was setting Korin up for... something.

"We—wizards, I mean—have all this power. It's so easy to abuse. That's why my ancestor created the wizard orders. That's why we have the laws we follow. The Knights—they thought they were better than that, that they could live outside the laws. And look what happened. Look what they did to the world."

Korin nodded, mutely. Afraid to say anything, afraid he might accidentally reveal he knew more about the knights and the origin of their corruption than he should.

"The problem is there are those among the wizard orders who also think themselves outside the laws. That they can get away with abuses of power, that no one will notice, or care, or have the power to stop."

"The church—" Korin began, but Sheluna shook her head.

"The blades are not the answer. Donatien...has his own agenda. Even if he had the same concerns, they don't always see what we do."

"I have no interest in becoming a spy."

"That's not at all what I'm asking."

It sounded very much like what she was asking. "Why are you talking about this with me? I'm not one of your wizards."

"No, but you are someone who reaches out. Who uses his magic, rather than just arguing about it. You…" She paused, studying him. "Surely you've noticed that even after the war, not everything is as it should be."

Korin kept his face blank, focused on his pulse, on his breathing, calling on magic to keep them steady. Was this some sort of trap? Did Sheluna know about the knife?

Her face showed no signs of suspicion, or even concern. But then, Sheluna knew a lot of the same tricks as Korin. Her body wouldn't betray her any more than his would. "What I'm looking for is allies, Korin. Wizards who believe in the same things I do— that magic is in the world to help, not to abuse. I don't want another war. No one does. But I'm afraid we may see one if nothing is done."

Korin most emphatically never wanted to see another war. Sheluna was right about that much. But whatever she was talking around, it couldn't be as harmless as she was trying to make it sound, or she would have come out and asked for…whatever she was asking for.

"You still haven't told me what it is you want."

Her eyes pulsed with scarlet light and her body tensed with frustration. "I don't *want* anything. Only to talk. To get to know you better."

Sheluna was an Archwizard, one who'd spent years studying and fighting against the knights. She'd been in Ulek. She'd seen the power of the knife, even if she didn't know exactly what she'd seen. As long as the knife was talking to Korin, haunting his dreams, he couldn't risk Sheluna's scrutiny. He couldn't afford to get that close.

"Thank you. I'm flattered. But I'm a healer, nothing more. I'm not the person you're looking for."

Sheluna spread her hands in a gesture of surrender. "It's your choice, of course." She stood, smoothing her robes. Cír moved noiselessly into the bushes as Sheluna gestured for Korin to precede her on the path back out into the garden.

As they came back into view, Sheluna tapped Korin's shoulder and he turned around to face her. "I'll be in Triome for a while," she said. "If you change your mind, you're welcome here."

Korin searched for a response that was politely noncommittal, but his thoughts derailed and he had to bite his lip against the mad grin that threatened to break free.

Across the garden—whistling as he walked—was Ádan.

THE UNEXPECTED SIGHT of Ádan sent a giddy feeling of happiness through Korin. He raised a hand to wave before it occurred to him he maybe shouldn't be so obvious about the fact that they knew each other.

But the movement caught Ádan's eye, and he smiled at Korin from across the garden and changed his path to angle towards Korin and Sheluna.

Ádan looked particularly good today. His sleeveless brocade jacket hung open, and he wore no shirt beneath. It made for a fine display of his chest and shoulders, a broad expanse of skin with muscles rippling beneath. He wasn't covered in jewels like most of the courtiers Korin had seen as he'd traversed the Palace this morn-ing, but Ádan had an attitude about him, an undeniable confi-dence, as though he didn't need such vulgar displays to prove he belonged.

Sheluna had also seen Ádan. Korin caught her eyes moving back and forth between them, wondered how much she saw.

As Ádan reached them, he gave a graceful bow. "Archwizard zhi Darkivel. Wizard Korin. What a delightful surprise."

"Apparently," Sheluna said, the glow of her eyes gone soft and speculative. "I see you two have met."

"Of course we have. I know everyone."

"Yes." Sheluna's tone had shifted back to dry. "I've noticed." To

Korin, she said, "Be warned, Korin, this one is Lysander's pet gossip. Be careful of him."

Ádan clutched his hands over his heart in an exaggerated gesture. "Truly, I'm wounded."

"You'll survive." Sheluna turned so she was facing Korin, with Ádan behind her. "Think about what I said. You have a great deal of potential. It would be a shame to see it go to waste," she added with a pointed sideways glance at Ádan.

Ádan bowed again as she walked away, but his smile was gone and the look he directed at her back was cold.

"Ádan, I—"

Ádan straightened and put a finger over Korin's lips. His face was still serious, but he winked. "Over here. Come on."

Ádan dragged Korin towards the nearest wall, into a decorative niche just large enough the two of them fit inside, hidden from anyone's view. Before Korin could say anything, Ádan hooked a finger in the open collar of Korin's shirt and pulled him forward into a kiss.

Korin leaned in, slid his hands under Ádan's vest, up the warm, bare skin of his back. He made a soft noise of protest when Ádan pulled away.

"Hi," Ádan said, grinning.

"Hi," Korin repeated, feeling a little dazed. Whatever he'd been planning to say was gone, so he went with, "I didn't expect to see you here."

"I could say the same. In fact, I will." He still had his fingers curled in Korin's shirt. His fingertips brushed lightly across Korin's sternum. "What were you doing taking to Sheluna?" The question sounded more worried than accusatory.

"She summoned me here," Korin answered. "She wants me to help her with…well, I'm not entirely sure. Wizard politics. I told her I wasn't interested."

"Good." Ádan lowered his voice, even though there was no one anywhere near. "You can't trust her."

It didn't escape Korin's attention that Sheluna had basically said the same thing about Ádan.

"The Darkivels are monsters," Ádan went on. "Sheluna and the Archduke—if it hadn't been for them—" Ádan's jaw clenched and he looked away, his entire body gone tense.

Korin put a hand on Ádan's shoulder and sent a soft ripple of soothing magic through him. "It's all right. I said no."

Ádan turned back with a smile that looked forced. "I know you did. I know you wouldn't—" He took a deep breath. "Sorry, it's been…" He shrugged.

Korin didn't entirely understand, but whatever was bothering Ádan, Korin was happy to distract him. "Come back to Marta's with me. Dinner was smelling delicious when I left."

Ádan visibly relaxed, his smile transitioning into something real. "That sounds perfect."

It sent a thrill through Korin, the fact that he could make Ádan smile like that. It evoked a bold, wicked feeling. What else could he make Ádan do? "Yes. Definitely. Let's go."

$\mathcal{D}$INNER *WAS* SMELLING delicious, the air full of coconut milk and spice as Korin and Ádan came in the front door. It was early yet; Lily was just getting the bar ready up front while Holli and Verania tended to the food. They all greeted Korin cheerfully, with extra smiles for Ádan as the two of them moved through the kitchen towards the stairs.

It occurred to Korin, the girls probably knew, or suspected, exactly what he and Ádan were getting up to in Korin's room. He tested that thought, waiting for the fluttery jolt of panic that had become so ingrained, living in the south.

There was a flare of anxiousness; his heartbeat sped up; his chest tightened. Then it let go. The girls were still smiling, Holli a little flushed as Ádan offered a flirty compliment. If they knew— and how could they not?—they didn't care.

Without noticing, he'd clenched his hands into a tight fist. Korin forced himself to relax. So many things were different here; he was still getting used to it all. So many things that he'd worried about all his life, and now...

They climbed the stairs to Korin's tiny room. It wasn't much, especially compared to the underground mansion that belonged to

Ádan and his friends, the wizard-knight safehouse that, even in its decay, was more opulent than any place Korin had ever been made welcome. But this was his. Korin's space, night after night after night. Where he was welcomed. Where it was assumed he would come home. Where he could have a guest whenever he liked.

Ádan toed the door closed behind him and Korin turned to slide into Ádan's arms, to resume the kiss they'd begun at the palace. Ádan's hands slid up Korin's back to wrap around his shoulders and cup the back of his head. Ádan's lips were soft, a relaxed, searching kiss that Korin was happy to surrender to.

It was nice to be able to relax. The first time he and Ádan had been together—well, first times were always fraught. The second time had been after he'd found out the truth about Ádan, still dazed and reeling from all that had happened that day. And the third time, night before last, he'd been so desperate to see Ádan again after his weeks away, he hadn't been of a mind to take anything slow. Tonight, though, for the first time, Korin felt no rush, no fear.

It was a new experience, and not just because it was with Ádan. It wasn't like Korin and Jonathan had ever had more than stolen moments, rushed and urgent. What would it have been like if Jon had been able to come to Triome?

Which was an awkward thought to have in the middle of kissing someone else. Korin pulled back, suddenly unsure.

Ádan's arms loosened enough to give Korin space, but didn't let go. "You're thinking deep thoughts," he said softly, brushing light fingers through Korin's hair.

"I can't seem to stop myself."

"It's all right. I like it when you think." His soft smile spread into a bright grin. "I like it when you do just about anything."

Ádan moved towards the bed and Korin let himself be drawn along. They settled side-by-side, backs against the wall, and Ádan put an arm around Korin's shoulder, pulling him close. "Anything you want to talk about?"

Not about Jon. How could Korin even be thinking about Jon? Jon wasn't here, and if he had been—would Korin trade away Ádan? What kind of a thought was that? This was nothing he could say to Ádan, so he flailed back to earlier concerns. "It's weird for me, being here with you," at Ádan's sardonic raised eyebrow, Korin hurried on, "and not being worried about anything. Nothing hanging over us. No threat or fear or need to rush."

A shadow flickered through Ádan's expression, quickly banished. But not so fast Korin didn't catch it. "What?" he asked.

Ádan shook his head. "It's nothing." At Korin's disbelieving look, his fingers tightened, pulling Korin closer. "Okay, not nothing. Just…an impossibility."

Korin fought down another burst of fear. "What's impossible?"

Ádan leaned his head down to rest his forehead against Korin's. His answer was delivered in a murmur. "I wish I could promise— that I could be that man who could say it will always be like this. That there will never be any threat or rush or…" He trailed off, closing his eyes.

Korin tilted his head to brush light kisses across Ádan's eyelids. "I don't want you to be that man or any other man. I want you to be you."

Ádan's words were a bare whisper. "You can't deny things would be easier if I'd been the person I was pretending to be."

They hadn't talked about this. By unspoken agreement, they'd avoided the topic while Korin was healing. Then Ádan had been away. Everything that hung in the air between them—Ádan's deception, the fact he was a knight, the power he was tied to, a guardian of.

The power that Korin was dreaming of. That might actually be reaching out to Korin, whispering to him in the night. But Korin *really* wasn't ready to talk about that.

"The one thing I can't deny is how I feel about you. I don't want you to be different because then you wouldn't be you, Ádan. And Ádan is the person I want to be here with."

. . .

KORIN'S WORDS had scored a sharp, painful cut into Ádan's heart. The fragile hope in Korin's voice. Korin felt safe here. When had he ever had that? Not in the war, certainly. Not, from what he'd described, in those years he'd spent on the road with his teacher.

What was Ádan bringing to his door? More danger. Threats Ádan himself didn't even understand yet.

Hard as he fought, Ádan couldn't get the image out of his head of Derian's body hanging, swinging gently in the wind. The creak of rope. Empty eye-sockets; skin ripped and torn.

This was the future that followed Ádan, shadowing his every step. Simply by being here, by existing in Korin's space, Ádan cast that shadow over him.

Derian was gone. No one had been able to protect him. In the depths of his heart, Ádan didn't expect there was a different future waiting for Varajas, for Nikki, for him. They would try their best, but the bitter, likeliest truth was that they would fail. They were probably going to die, and take how many others with them?

Ádan didn't believe it was in his power to protect the knife. He didn't know if it was in his power to protect his friends or himself. But maybe, just maybe, he could protect Korin.

Because if ever he had to look up at Korin's body swinging gently in the wind, or hear that same creaking or the ropes from which he hung...

Ádan swallowed the questions he'd been meaning to ask—about the blight, about the long-dead prince. Ádan could find another wizard to help. Or he'd figure out the answers himself. They hadn't gone through all the resources at the academy and safehouse yet. Perhaps a miracle would happen. Either way, he would keep Korin clear of it.

It was what Korin wanted. When Ádan had come to him right after they'd rescued him from the cultists—when they'd had that first chance to talk, clear-headed—Korin had been very clear he wanted nothing to do with the knife.

Korin wanted Ádan, but not the dangers Ádan dragged behind him. Ádan would find a way—somehow—to make it work. To give Korin security and safety and keep the horrors well clear of him.

If Ádan failed at everything else, he would keep Korin safe. Then, maybe, hopefully, the other dreams would stop. He wouldn't have to hear that creak creak creak. He wouldn't have to see—

"Did I say something wrong?" Korin asked, his voice rough with worry.

"No. Never," Ádan answered, knowing he had been quiet too long. He wrapped his arms around Korin and turned sideways, pulling them both down on the bed. "I want to be here with you, too.

"Always," Korin sighed, surrendering to Ádan's embrace, pliant in Ádan's arms.

"Always," Ádan repeated, knowing the promise was hollow.

The melancholy that had fallen between them was the opposite of what Ádan wanted. He shoved the unpleasant thoughts away as he rolled Korin onto his back and leaned down over him. He kissed the tip of Korin's nose, then his chin, then a light, teasing progress down Korin's pale throat. With gentle brushes of lips and tongue, he tickled the sensitive spot where neck met shoulder, knowing it would make Korin squirm.

That earned him a gasp and—what Ádan had been fishing for —a smile that brightened Korin's face until he was breathtaking. "Not fair," he said, the words belied by the laugh behind them. At the same time, Korin's fingers burrowed under Ádan's shirt to trail lightly up Ádan's side, and now it was Ádan squirming.

Then it was all-out war, as they both sought each other's sensitive spots, laughing as they wrestled. Predictably, the wrestling turned more sensual, as clothing was pushed aside and now skin pressed against skin.

They ground together, hands wrapped around each other, deep kisses joining them together so Ádan could taste Korin's moan as he climaxed. Ádan was not far behind, Korin's pleasure being its own stimulation.

After, they cleaned up, then returned downstairs for dinner. From then until much later, when they fell asleep on Korin's narrow bed, the talk was light and pleasant as Ádan did everything in his power to keep the weight of his responsibilities from falling down upon them both.

11

K ORIN STOOD IN the center of the Naktigan town square.

He wasn't really here. He'd never actually been here. Not in this precise spot, between the charred remains of two pyres that had long since burnt themselves out. He'd never seen the aftermath, the smoking remains. Which was how he knew this had to be a dream.

And yet, he could smell the acrid, greasy smoke. He felt the uneven crunch of charcoal embers beneath his feet. The silence was so oppressive it had to be real.

He hadn't thought of Naktigan in days. Hadn't dreamed of it since the night he'd told Ádan about what had happened here.

Now he was back.

A dream. No question. But it didn't feel like a dream. Nor did it feel unlike a dream. Confusing and unsettling and Korin wished he would simply wake up.

Instead, he looked to his left, to the pyre that had been at the center of the square. The piled wood had burned down to a thick layer of ash, but the pole at the center still stood. It was charred and pitted by the fire, but that wasn't the only reason it cast an uneven silhouette against the night sky. The round shape a few feet up, black with soot, but unmistakable. A skull.

Teriad's skull.

Korin picked his way through the ashes until he stood at the pole. The wood had been piled high when they'd tied Teriad in place. His skull was almost out of reach. Korin had to stand up on his toes, careful not to lean against the pole, which was no longer anchored. He pulled gently, working it unstuck without disturbing anything else.

Skull in hand, he moved away from the center of the square. As he walked, he brushed away ash and soot. The heat of the fire had cleansed the bone, leaving it brittle and scorched.

Still, it was a piece of Teriad. Not that long ago, it had *been* Teriad.

Once, early in his apprenticeship, Korin had asked the question that had seemed so obvious to his seventeen-year-old self. If healing was simply a matter of making the body remember when it had been healthier, why was death a barrier? Wasn't it just another condition they could reach back through and fix?

Teriad had been angry. It was one of the few times he'd ever yelled. That kind of magic was blasphemy, he'd said. It was dangerous. It was a corruption of what they did.

Korin never brought it up again. But now, standing here in this dream that wasn't entirely a dream, Korin wondered.

Teriad had been a hands-on kind of teacher. Korin and Lia had practiced their magic on him, on each other, on themselves. It meant that Korin knew Teriad's body in that deep, thorough way that he knew his own. Why couldn't he reconstruct that? It would take power and skill, but Korin's experience with the blight, with the cultists, was making him think he maybe had those in abundance.

But what happened next? Even if he were able to marshal the

power, to reach into Teriad's skull and pull his healthy body back through—what then? Would it even be Teriad?

Korin had never thought much about the question of souls, about what happened after death. He was mostly concerned with keeping people alive. He knew what the church taught—that good servants of the Light were taken into its presence when they died, and bad servants went…elsewhere. But that was predicated on a big assumption, that there was even a part of you that continued to exist once the body died.

Korin had seen no evidence, either way.

You are not the first to ask these questions.

The voice didn't surprise Korin. A part of him had been expecting it all along. The tree—the knife—the snake—Korin turned, ready to face it.

Tonight, she was none of those things.

A woman stood in the center of the square. Silver-pale in the moonlight, in a dress of shimmering, diaphanous white. She was beautiful, like the edge of a knife or a cobra poised to strike. Her white hair trailed behind her like a veil, reaching all the way to the ground. Her eyes glittered, diamond-white.

Everything in this dreamspace was strange. Which made it easier for Korin to ask, "Do you know the answers?"

Not when you ask the questions wrong.

"What does that mean?"

It means that you are a mortal being and I am not, so the answers I have would be neither useful nor relevant to you. Her voice took on a tone that Korin could only describe as rueful. **I have tried to give answers before, and have been told they were unhelpful.**

It was strange, having this conversation in this space. "You made all this happen. The least you could do is try to help me fix it."

She moved towards him, her steps gliding over the uneven

ground. Korin took a step back, unsure, his hand wrapping protectively around Teriad's skull.

She stopped a few feet away. **You loved him.**

"I did. Can you understand that?"

I understand what it is to love. And I understand what it is to lose that which you have loved.

"It was your power that did this. They sent your power against this town. These people who had already suffered so much. It was your power that drove them over the edge."

No.

The anger in that single word dimmed the moonlight and twisted the air so Korin had to struggle to breathe. He gasped, backing away again.

They took what was mine. They held me trapped, locked away in a prison. Forever, they have used me. It was not *my* power. It was stolen.

Korin felt it—her rage against the knights. It echoed his own.

But still, her claim that it wasn't her power—she might not have been in control of it, but Korin had stood in the room with the knife. He'd felt exactly the power that lived there. It was death. She was death. "They can't set you free."

Their words, you speak. Why would you listen to them? Look around you, Korin. This is what *they* have done. You hold Teriad in your hands because of *them*. You know this. *You know it.* Still you blame me.

Korin had seen the power of the knife unleashed. The black fog that had rolled down from the castle. It had spread through this town, reaching to engulf people with an almost living malevolence. Screams had echoed through the streets as people were drawn into it, as their bodies dissolved from the outside in.

So many dead, and the rest driven to a frenzy. Because of that, Teriad, Lia, and Jonathan were now all dead. Korin's family—gone.

"What do you want from me?"

Her anger faded and Korin could breathe free again. A heavy sadness came over her face. **I don't want to be alone.**

That sadness, that loneliness was thick enough Korin could feel it. And he understood this too. So hard not to feel for her, even knowing what she was. This was a suffering anyone would be able to identify with.

But he couldn't trust her. He couldn't listen. Not while he stood here, in the place where so many had died because of her.

"I'm sorry." He set Teriad's skull down, placing it with delicate care on the ground. Even if this was a dream, no reason not to be careful. "I wish I could help you."

A dream. Nothing but a dream. It had to be a dream. Which meant he could wake up.

KORIN OPENED HIS EYES. Ádan was still asleep beside him. The dream had been terrible, but at least Korin had dreamed quietly.

He considered waking Ádan up, telling him everything that had just happened. Confessing that the knife had been talking to Korin. That the knife had been invading his dreams.

The trouble was, that conversation led to so many more things. The knife had been correct when she'd said that Korin was still angry at the knights. That he still blamed them for so many things. Somehow, someday, he was going to have to face that, to reconcile it with the fact that Ádan was one of them.

There were excuses Korin could make—had made—that helped him avoid the issue. The fact that Ádan had been here, rather than Ulek. That he hadn't been on the front lines of the war. The knights had done horrible things, but Ádan had been separate from that.

Once they started talking about it, though, they'd have to *talk* about it. Korin wasn't ready for that. Not yet.

The knife was talking to him, yes. Even haunting his dreams.

That was fine. Korin was fine. It wasn't hurting him. The discussion about it could wait.

Korin leaned in and brushed a light kiss across Ádan's lips, smiling as Ádan gave a soft sigh and curved closer to Korin. This was good, right here, and Korin wasn't about to disturb that.

Closing his eyes, Korin fell back asleep, and passed the rest of the night without any further dreams.

12

*A*NOTHER DAY BROUGHT more people seeking Korin's aid, and in and among the coughs and fevers and sprains was another person who had been healed by Korin before —a person who had been injured again by magic.

Ádan had stuck around for breakfast, but had left soon after, saying he needed to check in with Nikki and Varajas. Korin considered going to the safehouse to ask all three what they thought about this new phenomenon, but in the end, it was wizard business and Korin needed wizard advice.

Sadly, the one wizard he knew wasn't much help. "I don't know what to tell you, Korin."

Renée was at her shop today, organizing and cataloging. Korin's offer of help had been immediately accepted and now he was walking behind her with a box as she pulled random objects off crowded shelves and dropped them in with no rhyme or reason Korin could track.

"Someone is doing this on purpose. I'm sure of it."

"I'm certain you're right."

"But who? And why?"

Renée was examining a bundle of springs that seemed tangled

together beyond recovery. She frowned, turning the lump this way and that, before shrugging and throwing it in the box. "I don't have any more information for you today than I did the last time we had this discussion."

The box was starting to get heavy, but all it took was a line of energy into his arms, his shoulders, and his back, and the pressure was gone. "People are getting hurt. Whoever this is, if they want to come after me, they should come after *me*. There's no excuse and no reason for them to be making other people suffer."

"It certainly is suggestive, though, isn't it?" Renée murmured.

Korin stepped back, pulling the box out from under her hand and forcing her to look at him. "What does that mean?"

"Maybe nothing. Maybe everything. But I'll tell you this much, kiddo. If I were trying to craft some plan to upset you personally, to throw you off balance, I'd definitely aim it at other people rather than directly at you."

"So you're saying…"

"If you pay attention, you'll note I'm carefully not saying anything. I don't *know* anything for certain. But I can't think of any possible explanation that's good for any of us."

This was the problem with Renée. There was only so far she was willing to speculate if she didn't have any actual evidence. Korin wanted to talk through possibilities, no matter how far-fetched. Renée held things close until she knew for certain.

The bell up front rang and Korin jumped. He'd never heard anyone actually come into the shop before. Renée flashed him a sideways smile and moved back towards her counter. He followed, box still in hand.

He was surprised by the wizard who emerged from the maze. Samir was here, along with his bat hanging upside-down from the arch of his staff. Samir showed no sign of being surprised by Korin, nodding at him as Samir approached Renée.

"Are you following me?" Korin asked.

The amused twitch of an eyebrow was the only break in Samir's otherwise perfectly schooled demeanor. He pointedly addressed Renée. "I'm here to pick up Sheluna's order."

"I figured." Renée took the box from Korin. "Wait here and I'll get her stuff together." Renée disappeared into the back, leaving Korin alone with Samir.

Who seemed every bit as impossibly perfect and untouchably unreal as he had yesterday. He was looking at Korin with a bland sort of curiosity. It had to be bland. Any more extreme expression would have ruined the smooth perfection of his face. Korin wondered if they would simply stand here in silence, staring at each other, until Renée returned, but then Samir asked, "Why would I be following you?"

"If Sheluna wanted…" Korin trailed off, realizing he had no ending for that sentence. If Sheluna wanted to know what Korin was doing, she had plenty of ways to accomplish that, as demonstrated by the birds that had first summoned him to her.

Samir waited with frustrating patience for Korin to complete his thought. The best Korin could manage was, "Clearly she sends you to run her errands."

"I had the time." Samir idly reached up to stroke his bat's head. "I offered. She's not like you think."

"You don't know what I think."

Samir lifted one shoulder in a shrug. "She's not like most people think." He continued to stroke his familiar.

"Your bat," Korin said, flailing for small talk, "is bigger than I've ever seen."

That brought what seemed to be a genuine smile to Samir's face. "She's a flying fox. Her name is Krys."

"Krys," Korin repeated. At the sound of her name, her eyes popped open and she craned her head around to look at him. "She knows her name," Korin murmured.

"Of course she does." The warmth in Samir's voice was unmistakable.

Korin knew little about the Wing's familiars. Teriad had

dismissed them as frivolous pets. A distraction from real magic. Teriad had dismissed a great deal of magic other orders pursued. Korin had learned to keep his curiosity to himself if it wasn't about healing.

That didn't mean any of his questions had gone away. Which made him think of Sheluna again. "Why is she interested in me? Why does she care what I do?"

Samir followed the change of subject without blinking. "She knew Teriad, and she knows you a little. At least, she was aware of the work you were doing in Ulek. She knows you're a capable wizard. That you're smart. She likes smart people."

"I'm sure she has plenty of those to choose from."

Samir lifted an eyebrow, gave Korin a flat look. "You'd be surprised."

At that moment, Renée returned, wrapped bundle in hand. She handed it to Samir. "Everything's in there."

"Thank you." Samir tucked the bundle under one arm, and gave a slight bow. "Wizard Renée. Wizard Korin. It has been a pleasure."

"I don't understand him," Korin admitted after Samir was out the door. "Or Sheluna."

"What's there to understand about Sheluna?" Renée sat down behind her counter, making no move towards returning to the work they'd been doing.

Korin realized he hadn't told Renée about his summons and his strange meeting. "She talked to me, the other day. She wants...I don't even know. She said she wanted to get to know me better."

Renée gave a thoughtful hum, but said nothing.

"You're being less than helpful again."

"I know." She leaned forward on her elbows, considering Korin. "The truth is, I'm not sure what to tell you. I have what I think is a perfectly natural suspicion of the Wing and the Darkivels, but..." She gave a deep sigh. "You keep bringing me questions I don't know the answers to, and quite honestly, I don't want to know the answer. The magic you do, it isn't my field, and I'm too old to be learning new tricks. Sheluna now, she might have your answers. Unless..."

"Unless?" Korin pressed when Renée didn't finish.

"Unless she's the one causing you trouble."

The Sheluna Ádan believed in would certainly be capable of that. But she would truly have to be a monster, to be able to go around undoing Korin's work—basically torturing people—and then sit down with Korin and talk about how wrong it was, wizards abusing their power. If she were really that person... Korin shuddered.

"Do you think that's true?" he asked.

"I don't know enough to say one way or the other. Which is why I didn't bring it up before."

Renée had, as she so often did, pulled out a piece of clockwork to fiddle with as she talked. Korin was ready to let the conversation move on, so he asked her about it. She began to talk about the new project with much more enthusiasm than she'd shown for discussing Sheluna.

All the while, though, the questions continued to circle in the back of Korin's mind. Who was Sheluna really? If she wasn't behind the attacks, could she help him? And if she was...was Korin ready to face down an Archwizard?

13

*Á*DAN LOOKED UP as Varajas came into the study with yet another stack of books. "Where did you find those?"

"Don't ask," Varajas said, dropping them onto the growing mound of to-be-reads. V's clothes were filthy with dirt and cobwebs and a layer of dust had turned V's dark copper skin to gray.

Across the table from Ádan, Nikki made a disgusted face. He pointed. "Are those worms?"

Varajas glared coldly at him. "Ádan said to find all the books. I have now found *all* the books."

The last few days had been dedicated to searching—first through the safehouse, which was easy, and then through the ruins of the Academy, which was...messier. Anything they could find with writing in or on it. Records, journals, histories, pamphlets—even small stashes of fiction that various knights and recruits had tucked in hidden nooks and crannies.

This study was never going to be the same. Fine hardwood furniture that had probably cost a fortune to import from the south was now covered in the dust and grime of the moldering books piled high on every surface.

Nikki held out his hand and the—yes, worms—crawling on the surface of several of the books Varajas had just deposited erupted into tiny flames, twisting and turning black until they crumbled to nothing.

Varajas sat down heavily on the remaining chair at their table. "Oh yes, that's brilliant. Let's set things on fire in the huge pile of paper we've just created."

"Oh is this bothering you?" Another burst of fire, this time closer to V.

"Enough," Ádan said firmly. The two of them had been bickering like this for days. It was mostly boredom and proximity and the stress they all were feeling, but if he let it continue, it could escalate into real conflict. "Nothing gets better from us fighting with each other."

"Who died and made you—" Nikki stopped, his face turning bright red. The playground taunt wasn't so funny anymore.

Ádan ignored it and went back to reading.

Not that the book in front of him was particularly compelling. A bound ledger from two hundred years ago, mostly tracking food and other supplies moving in and out of the Academy. Grain and meat and fruit, weapons, raw iron, wood. Line after line of expenses and payments with the occasional note about a new trade agreement.

So boring, Ádan could barely focus, but he couldn't put it down till he'd read through every list. He couldn't afford to miss a single hint, even the most oblique reference, that pointed at the knowledge he was after.

Nikki slammed his own book closed. "This is pointless."

This, too, was an argument that had been ongoing. And every time, Ádan responded with, "We don't know that."

Ádan hadn't looked up from his book, but out of the corner of his eye, he caught Nikki and Varajas exchanging a look, one he could read easily enough. They'd been having this conversation without him.

They didn't have all the facts. To be fair, that was because Ádan hadn't shared all the facts. But things were bleak enough already. Everyone was snapping at each other. The last thing anyone needed was for Ádan to admit that he'd been given charge of the knife, but that it wouldn't talk to him. That Derian had warned Ádan that knife would creep into his dreams and whisper to him in his waking hours, and that he had to be on guard for its lies and its manipulations but—jokes on everyone! Ádan didn't have to worry about any of those things because he hadn't been able to forge the connection he was supposed to have. He had failed in that one, central part of his duty.

He'd have to confess that he'd already failed and he didn't have the first idea why.

"Let's be realistic." Varajas's voice had that careful, patient quality of a person talking to a particularly stubborn toddler. "Even if some knight before us wrote down anything about the knife and what it is and what we should do with it—which they probably didn't—and even if that information happens to be in one of the few random books they didn't drag to Ulek when they fled—which it won't be—it still won't be enough. None of us—not even you, Ádan—understand this magic. And my suspicion is Derian didn't either. And not the Grandmaster who came before him, or the Grandmaster who came before that. That's how we got to this place."

Nikki took over. "The knife got to all of them. It destroyed us. The Darkivels, the church—they would never have been able to do it if we hadn't already been broken. Now there's just three of us, and if the answer to how to survive this stewardship were in a book, I suspect someone would already have read it."

"So what, then?" Ádan demanded. "If you have a better idea, I'd love to hear it."

Another look passed between them, one that promised Ádan wasn't going to like what came next. "Two things," Nikki said. "First, we need to go to Ulek."

Ádan snapped his answer. "I've been to Ulek."

Varajas, still patient, "We need to go back. You want to dig through books? Fine, but if there actually is something useful to find, it's not going to be here. It's going to be there. Beyond that, there could be survivors still. People who escaped, who hid. If there's anyone at all…."

It was the truth Ádan had been trying to avoid for weeks. "Wishing there were more than three of us isn't going to make it true."

"Which is why we want to mount a serious search," V said. "Now that the wizards and the church have backed off—we know our hiding places better than they do. We have a better chance of finding anyone who's left."

Ádan closed his book, leaned back in his chair. "It's wishful thinking. It's dangerous even to hope. We can't plan for the future based on the chance someone else escaped."

"We need help!" Nikki slammed his hand on the table. "The three of us aren't enough. Tell me you can see that."

"It's what we have." Ádan resisted raising his voice. "It's all we have. We have to find a way to make it work."

"That's the other thing," V said. "The second thing we need to talk about. If there isn't understanding to be found in these books —in any books—then either we need to learn a lot about magic that none of us know. Or…we need to recruit someone who already does."

Someone who understood this kind of magic. "You're talking about Korin."

"Yes."

"No," Ádan answered immediately. "Korin doesn't want to be involved. He's said as much."

"Korin's already involved," Nikki said. "Thanks to you. He already knows our secrets. And we all saw what he can do against the blight—against those people who were tapped into the knife's power."

"We've already put our trust in him," Varajas added.

Ádan stood so fast he almost knocked his chair over backwards. In that moment, he didn't see the room or his friends anymore. Only a body—Derian's body—rotting as it hung. "No. I'm not dragging Korin in. That's final. We'll find someone else."

"Who?" Nikki demanded.

"I don't know. Another wizard we can trust. Or I'll learn the magic somehow. Or maybe you're right and we'll find a survivor— someone who knew more than we do."

Derian's body swinging. The creak of the rope. Ádan heard it. Ádan saw it. Except it wasn't Derian's body hanging, was it?

It was Korin's.

"I will find a way," Ádan spoke clearly and carefully. "I'll find an answer. One that doesn't put—" *Korin* "anyone else in danger."

"What if that answer doesn't exist?" Varajas asked gently.

Ádan was resolute. "I'll find it."

"But—" Nikki started.

Ádan was done. He had to get out. Away from this argument. Away from this underground tomb and the dead men who had lived here. Away from the knife. Away from everything.

"I'll give you an update as soon as I have one," he said sharply. And walked out.

What Ádan needed more than anything right now was Korin. He needed to see Korin, to touch him, to remind himself that Korin was all right. That Korin was safe.

Fortunately, Korin was easy to find. He wasn't at Marta's, but Ádan's next stop was Renée's shop, where the two wizards were in the back, drinking coffee and talking intently. They fell quiet as he got close, but as soon as Ádan came in sight around the shelves, Korin brightened. "Ádan!"

"Hey, Sunshine. Wizard Renée."

Renée gave him a nod. Then, to Korin, said, "I can see that you're done with me now. You boys run along. I've got work to do."

Outside, Ádan dragged Korin into the narrow alley between Renée's shop and the next, pressed him against the wall, and kissed him thoroughly. He pulled back to Korin's smile.

"Hi," Korin said, sounding a little dazed.

"Hi." Somehow, everything seemed easier, better, just being here with Korin. "You got any plans tonight?"

Korin shook his head, still smiling.

"Good. I was hoping for a quiet evening at your place. If that's all right."

"That can probably be arranged." Korin took his hand, pulled him towards the street.

Ádan followed, knowing this wasn't a solution to anything. Knowing he was only avoiding his real problems. But needing this all the same. Besides, he wasn't going to find any answers tonight, no matter what he did. So he might as well take the escape while he could.

14

*A*LL PLANS FOR a quiet evening evaporated once they got to Marta's.

The late-afternoon regulars were just settling in, which meant Verania was moving through the barroom, delivering drinks. As soon as Korin came in, she waved him over. "There's a message came for you. Said it's urgent. Someone sick."

"I'm sorry," Korin said to Ádan, "But I have to—"

"Of course you do." Ádan elbowed Korin gently in the arm. "I'll tag along and we can grab some food after."

The note with the address was in the kitchen. Korin looked at it, frowned. He'd been there before. "Who brought this?" he asked Verania. "Did they say what was wrong?"

One of the side effects of Korin's work over the past few weeks was that Verania—all the workers at Marta's—had become far less squeamish about discussing symptoms of illness or injury. "Coughing up blood. Trouble breathing. Firstborn girl. Young, nervous thing. Talking about her dad. Said the consumption had come back."

Korin wasn't imagining things. "I remember her. And her father." He crumpled the note. "It *can't* come back. I *healed* him."

"Is something going on?" Ádan asked.

Korin realized he'd talked to Renée about this, but not Ádan. "I'll explain on the way."

It wasn't that Korin wanted to keep secrets from Ádan. It was only that as they walked, as Korin filled Ádan in on the strange recurrences of injuries he'd fixed, Ádan lost his playful expression, became serious, worried. This wasn't at all what Korin wanted to make Ádan feel.

Ádan came immediately to the same conclusion Renée had. "Someone's doing this on purpose."

"Yes, I figured that much out. But who? And why?"

Korin half expected Ádan to jump in with an accusation of Sheluna, but instead, Ádan stayed thoughtfully silent for a full block of walking. Then he said, "My first question would be—is this happening just to people you've healed? Or are those just the only victims you've seen so far, because they already knew to come to you."

That question had never even occurred to Korin. His stomach twisted as he moved from embarrassed he had assumed it was all about him to horrified at the thought there could be a whole wave of magically hurt and injured he didn't even know about. "Why would anyone do that?"

"No reason that's good." Ádan's mouth set into a determined line. "We'll just have to figure it out."

Ádan's easy *we* relaxed some of Korin's tension. Even Renée, while she'd been happy to talk about it, hadn't offered to help. Ádan made it sound like his assistance was a given. The only question was, "How?"

"If we knew the right magic…" Ádan trailed off into a tense silence.

Which seemed strange. In their brief time together, Korin had seen Ádan cheerful, had seen him confident. Korin had seen worried, determined, suspicious. In all those moods, the one constant was that Ádan kept talking. "Is something wrong?"

Ádan shook his head. "Nothing you need to worry about."

Korin opened his mouth to press, to insist that he was here for Ádan, but then he closed it again. It wasn't true, was it? He'd told Ádan he didn't want anything to do with the knights and the knife they were still trying to protect. If Ádan was keeping things from Korin, it was him doing as Korin had asked.

What kind of a friend did that make Korin? Here Ádan was doing what he could to help Korin out, when he had so many other things to worry about, and Korin couldn't be bothered to do the same for him. Guilt stabbed at Korin's stomach.

Was it wrong of Korin to wish for peace? To be able to leave all the horrible things behind him?

Too many questions with no answers, and Korin was no closer to figuring it out by the time they arrived at their destination.

THE FIRST THING Korin did as they entered the sick household was check mother, daughter, and grandchild for any signs of the disease. Consumption was a brute of a disease that spread through households like lightning once someone was at the coughing stage.

Last time, Korin had done this same thing and found nearly all of them infected. He'd cleaned the invasive illness from their blood before sending them away to work on the father.

This time, they were clean.

"Don't get too close," Korin cautioned Ádan as they moved into the room where the father had been loosely quarantined. "You can breathe this from the air." Korin wasn't too worried. Most wizard-trained were more resistant to getting sick than non-magic types, and Korin could heal Ádan as easily as he could anyone—easier, really—but better if he didn't need to.

The firstborn man was visibly sick again. His lips were flaked with dried blood. His face was bright with fever even as he shivered under three different blankets. He was coughing weakly. The eyes he turned to Korin were glassy. "It's all right," Korin reassured him. "I'm going to make you better again." But in the man's fevered state, he didn't seem to hear.

From the doorway, Ádan asked, "Could he have been infected again by someone else?"

"It's possible for that to happen." Korin sat down carefully on the edge of the bed. "But he wouldn't have progressed this far this fast." Korin wiped the blood from the man's mouth with gentle fingers. "This disease—it attacks the lungs. Destroys them. But that takes time. I rebuilt his insides." It had been a real challenge, but Korin had done it. "He couldn't be sick again like this—not this fast. Not without someone doing this on purpose."

Ádan nodded, his expression thoughtful.

Korin lay a hand on the man's chest, reached in with magic awareness. Found a body ravaged in exactly the same way as it had been before.

What he didn't find was any sign of the disease.

Korin pulled back out. Looked at Ádan. "He isn't sick."

Ádan raised an eyebrow. "I hate to argue with the expert, but…he looks pretty sick to me."

"He's…hurt. Someone forced his body back to the way it was when he *was* sick. But there's no disease in him. None of the infection."

"I don't understand," Ádan said. "How can he be sick without being sick?"

Teriad would have understood. Any Staff wizard would. But Korin didn't have time right now to give a full lesson in epidemiology. "We get sick because things inside us make us sick. Tiny invaders. It's complicated. He had those before—the bacteria causing the disease. Now he doesn't. There's no reason he should be like this."

Except that his body had been like this before Korin put him back together. In the same way it was the easiest magic in the world for Korin to heal a recently broken bone—because the body still clearly remembered what it was like to be whole—could someone push a recently healed body back into sickness because the body still remembered being sick?

The answer was yes. The real question—still—was *why*?

I can help, came the soft, whispering voice in Korin's mind.

Korin kept very still, tried to keep his face from showing anything. He carefully formed the words in his head. *What do you mean?*

The knife answered. **The magic used here is my magic. I can find the one who used it. Let me in.**

I don't want to hurt this man. I want to heal him.

He is already hurt. I need to touch him. To feel through him.

Korin risked a glance at Ádan, but Ádan's attention was focused on the sick man. He didn't seem to have noticed anything different with Korin. Probably wouldn't notice if Korin let the knife do as she wanted.

If Korin could trust her. *Why would you help me?*

Why wouldn't I?

That's not good enough.

I want to help. Softer. **I don't want to be alone. No one should have to be alone. Not you, not me. Not the one who is doing this. I can feel them reaching for me, like a child searching for its mother.**

Korin shuddered as a wave of cold washed through him. The knife called Korin her child, but she'd talked about others as well. Including… *The cultists. The ones who tried to kill me. Are there more? Are they the ones doing this?*

The ones who tried to kill you are dead.

Korin wasn't sure she understood his question. Either way, it didn't matter. In the fragile state this man was in, the power of the knife would kill him. *I'm a healer. You are not. You can't help me here.*

The knife withdrew. Korin could feel her pulling back out of his mind, but she gave one last whisper before she was gone. **Be** careful. **The one who did this has power. Perhaps more than you.**

Korin focused on healing. He flooded power into the old man, where he had been broken, then healed, then broken again. It was harder this time, the magic back-and-forth causing its own trauma. The man's heart, his lungs, they were going to come out of this weaker than before. Whatever this game was some other wizard was playing, it was causing real damage. Korin was done with it.

Korin opened his eyes. Ádan watched him, studying Korin's face. He raised his eyebrows in an unspoken question. Korin shook his head a little. He didn't want to talk here, not in front of the people who had come to him for help.

The people who had trusted Korin. Who had put themselves in Korin's hands, in good faith. Because of that, they'd been drawn into the center of a conflict that had nothing to do with them. Someone had used them, without any thought for the consequences.

Korin squirmed his way through the family's thanks and got out the door with Ádan as quickly as he could.

"What's wrong?" Ádan asked once they were away.

"I'm sick of this. These people did nothing but come to me for help, and they're getting punished for it." Korin's anger was authentic, even if it wasn't the whole story. He wasn't entirely comfortable with the conversation he'd had with the knife with Ádan right there in the room with him.

But that conversation had given him something. "Whoever is doing this is powerful." That wasn't unreasonable information for Korin to have figured out himself. Ádan didn't need to know where that knowledge had come from. "Maybe more than me. And knows this magic."

Ádan's expression hardened as he reached the same conclusion Korin had. "Sheluna. You think this is Sheluna."

"I think it's time to find out."

"I'm going with you." Ádan's tone was resolute.

Korin wanted to do the mature thing and remind Ádan how risky that was for him, how much he couldn't afford Sheluna's close scrutiny. But in truth, Korin wanted Ádan next to him. Wanted that support. So he nodded and took Ádan's hand. Gave it a squeeze. "Thank you."

They turned together towards the road that would lead to the palace.

WITH ÁDAN AT HIS SIDE, Korin had no trouble getting into the palace. He was more concerned about access to Sheluna's private garden, but either the guards remembered him from earlier or they were simply accustomed to wizards coming and going. No one made any move to stop him as he climbed back to the rooftop garden where Sheluna was holding court.

This time, he walked boldly forward, ignoring the other wizards, the familiars, and even the tiger that sat up at Korin and Ádan's approach.

Sheluna was seated with two other wizards—Samir and someone Korin didn't know. She waved them away at Korin's approach. Her strange red eyes began to glow softly. Korin didn't know what to read from that, but he refused to be intimidated.

"Was it all a lie?" He demanded. It was easy to be brave with Ádan's solid presence right behind. "All your talk of things not being right, of not letting wizards abuse their power. Is this a game to you?"

Korin watched her face for every move, every twitch. Her brows pulled together in what seemed to be honest confusion. If she was feigning, she was doing it well. But then, Korin expected Archwizard Sheluna zhi Darkivel to be an expert at lying.

"Whatever accusation you're here to make," she said in a cool voice, "I'm afraid I'm going to need more information."

Samir had taken a step forward, and the tiger's attention on

Korin had sharpened. Everyone was watching him. Ádan, at his back, was tense.

"Someone is hurting people." Korin kept his voice even and calm. "Someone—a wizard—has been undoing the healing that I have done."

Again, he studied Sheluna's face, but saw no change in her expression, no ripple of anything that could be read as evasion or guilt. So either she was honestly surprised or she was good enough to hide her deception from Korin.

Either was possible.

"Why come to me with this?" Her voice, her neutral expression, neither gave any hint of what she might be thinking. "Why bring these accusations to my doorstep?"

"Because the list of people capable of this magic is very short." Korin paused, giving plenty of time for those words to sink in. Then came right out and said it. "And you would be at the top of it."

Rustling all around. He had the full attention of everyone in the garden. Everyone was poised, waiting to see how Sheluna would respond.

Her eyes flashed brighter. The light seemed an angry color, but her voice maintained its utter calm. "I can see how you would think that, but I assure you I have better things to do with my time. As for the rest of my order." Her voice got slightly louder, pitched to carry through the entire garden. "If I find out any Wing wizard is involved in such abuses, they will be sorry the Blades didn't find them first." The threat was delivered in a mild tone, but it sent a shiver through Korin.

Still, "How can I know you're telling the truth?"

Silence fell as Sheluna considered him, tapping a finger against her lips thoughtfully. The glow of her eyes softened, and she stood. "All of you, leave me." She aimed the command at the garden, at the other Wing wizards milling about. They departed—many with visible reluctance—until it was only Sheluna, Korin, Samir, and Ádan remaining.

Still standing, Sheluna asked, "Do you genuinely want the truth?"

"Of course," Korin answered. "Why else would I be here?"

Samir opened his mouth, but at sharp look from Sheluna, closed it again. "We will give you the benefit of the doubt." She was talking about Korin, but her words seemed aimed at Samir, and he remained silent.

Now she turned her attention directly to Korin. "Am I to presume you came here directly from helping one of these people?"

The question seemed safe enough. "Yes."

"Good. It's fresh in your mind. Now listen. When you heal, you are reaching back through the body's memory. Searching for signs of change. Yes?"

Korin nodded, unsure where this was going.

"Yes. If you extend that same sense to yourself, you can feel the traces of the magic you used. It's harder to find. You have to listen very carefully, but it's there."

She stopped, watching Korin expectantly. Like she expected him to try it now.

He still wasn't sure why she was telling him this, but it was interesting nonetheless. Korin closed his eyes, reached into himself like he was trying to heal.

At first, he felt nothing new. His body was familiar, with a history he knew well. If magic had a feel, a trace, he wasn't seeing it.

He peeked one eye open. Sheluna was watching him, waiting, but there was an air of patience about her. She wanted him to figure this out, for some reason. He took another deep breath, refocused.

The old man. Korin could remember what it felt like healing him. The flow of power, the way it had moved. The extra care he'd had to take.

The magic had felt a certain way as it worked through his patient, but Korin had felt it in himself as well. A tingle in his fingers. A warmth in his chest. Those were signals, but they were a way in. Korin reached deeper, focused in with all the intensity that he usually focused out.

There. There it was. Fleeting. Ephemeral. But he'd found it.

"Yes," Sheluna murmured. "Good. You see it."

How could she tell? This was fascinating, a whole new idea Korin wanted to explore. He wanted to ask more questions. To dig into this new concept.

Until he remembered why he was here. His suspicions. "Yes. I see it. Now what?"

"You turn that sight outward. You know the magic you used. You have the key. Now you're looking for the lock. To see if I'm the one who created the situation that you countered."

The difficulty, the complexity of what she was suggesting—Korin didn't know whether to be flattered that she thought he could just do it, or annoyed that she, the Archwizard, seemed to think what was easy for her was easy for everyone.

Then he felt it, the light touch against his lower back. Ádan's movement hidden between them, where no one else would see. It was wordless support, encouragement. Belief.

So Korin reached out. He twisted the magic in his mind, sinking into the feel of it, then felt for that same essence in Sheluna, the matching energy.

Everyone waited, silent, as Korin felt his way through this new idea, tried to make it work.

"I can't feel it," he finally said. He opened his eyes, met her assessing gaze. "Which could be that I'm still not doing it right." He felt the need to say that, to make sure everyone understood that was a possibility.

"You'll get there." Sheluna spoke with the confidence Korin didn't feel. "You picked the first part up quickly. The rest will come."

She sounded like she meant it. Korin had to fight not to squirm at the compliment. He changed the subject. "If it isn't you, then, who could be doing this?"

Sheluna's eyes flashed again. "If it's any of my wizards, I promise you, I'll find out."

Korin wanted to trust her. He wanted to believe her. "If you do find out, please tell me. I want to know people are safe."

She nodded. It felt like a dismissal. Korin was happy to take the opportunity to escape.

Outside, he fell back against a wall, scrubbed his face with his hands. Ádan leaned back next to him, their shoulders touching. "You're brave, Sunshine." Ádan pressed in. "But maybe we should talk about less aggressive approaches in the future."

"I was angry," Korin admitted from behind his hands.

"I know. And I have to admit, I found it pretty glorious. That is, in the moments when I wasn't convinced she was going to turn us into rocks."

Korin peeked out between his fingers. The more time he spent with Ádan, the better he got to know him, the faster he recognized this flippant tone, the demons-may-care smile. This was Ádan putting on a front. "I'm sorry. I really didn't think."

Where their arms hung together, Ádan caught Korin's fingers, gave them a quick squeeze. "Don't worry about it. Everything's fine."

Korin wasn't sure that was true, but he didn't want to argue. "What she did give me was maybe a way to find the person who's doing all this."

Korin hadn't been able to lock in his sense of Sheluna, but he believed that the magic she'd shown him was genuine. Maybe, just maybe, he could make it work without the pressure of her and Samir watching him.

"I'm game," Ádan said. What had Korin ever done to deserve such unwavering support?

"I'll need someplace quiet, and maybe private."

Ádan led him into one of the gardens, to a corner where they were surrounded by high bushes and draping trees and the only sounds Korin could hear were soft bird-calls and a fountain trickling somewhere close.

Without Sheluna watching, Korin took his time. He felt his way back to the state where he could feel those threads of his own magic, of the change he'd brought to the world. Slowly, carefully, he tried to twist it around to what Sheluna had been talking about.

He was too far away. Too much time had passed. He had a theoretical idea how he could use this to track the culprit, but it simply wasn't possible right now. Not unless he wanted to wait for another victim.

I can help.

Again, the knife's offer of help. *How?* Korin asked.

We both touched the old man. I can reconnect you.

Korin didn't trust the offer any more now than he had before. *You seem very eager to help.*

I am not what they think I am.

Was it worth the risk? If he could stop the next person from suffering. If he could find the person who was committing these atrocities. Repeated trauma, the back and forth was hard on people. Not just emotionally, but snapping back and forth, even with Korin's healing—one of these people he might not be able to fix again.

Okay, Korin thought. *Help me.*

The knife's energy moved through Korin like a fever, burning and chills all at once. He was spinning, falling, drowning. The city pressed in around him, thousands of burning embers of life that he could suddenly feel. He rushed through them, dragged along by the vise-grip of the knife's power, until his mind filled with a single star and it engulfed him.

This was the old man. He was familiar. True to her word, the knife had brought Korin back.

But if Korin had been hoping for the chance to be slow and

careful, to explore this new magic, he wasn't going to do it. Korin and the knife were twined together, and they were both here, both their magic sunk deep. Sight attuned, Korin could see the reaching threads of decay spreading out from them.

Stop! Korin tried to fight back, to heal the new hurt as it expanded, but with the knife's magic inside him, his own power felt distant and strange.

It was like the blight all over again, thick tendrils of destructive energy moving through this man, alive and searching and hungry. Except this time Korin wasn't fighting it. He was *causing* it.

Let him go! Stop it!

I can't. This is what they have made me. But look.

Another surge of power, and with it came understanding. Korin felt the connection, strands of a web reaching out from the tree, through him, through the old man, and out into the world. Other magic, as cold and corruptive as the knife. It was close.

With that, the knife pulled back and Korin snapped back into himself. Her sudden absence left Korin hollow and aching, and far too aware of what he'd just done.

That man had trusted Korin, had put himself in Korin's hands, in good faith, believing Korin wouldn't abuse that trust. Korin had used him. Without any thought for the consequences, he had invited in a power he didn't understand.

No, that was a lie. Korin knew the knife's power. He'd seen it in Ulek. He'd seen it in the blight. He'd seen it in the corruption that had spread through the people who had tried to kill him just a few weeks ago.

Korin had let his guard down, and someone else had gotten hurt.

"What's wrong?"

Korin's eyes opened at Ádan's question. Too much to ask that Ádan wouldn't notice Korin's discomfort. Ádan had been able to read Korin since the first day they'd met. "The magic was…"

His throat closed around the words, and Teriad's voice echoed in Korin's mind. *I can't forgive this.*

If Ádan said that to Korin, Korin might die.

"It doesn't matter," Korin said. "I think it worked. I found the person who's been doing this."

Korin braced for more questions. If Ádan asked again, he would tell the truth. But Ádan only nodded, taking Korin's hands. "Let's go find this asshole."

15

ORIN FOLLOWED THE thread of power out of the palace, but he didn't turn towards the lower city. It was leading him somewhere close, somewhere in cliffside. Ádan didn't question the direction, following silently. Once again, Korin worried about Ádan's silence, but he wasn't exactly in a position to press Ádan to open up.

They pushed deeper into the neighborhood than Korin had previously explored, through rows of mansions where liveried guards eyed Korin with suspicion, even with Ádan in his noble dress at Korin's side.

Korin turned down a road that led between two estates and then farther, out past what seemed like it might be the edge of the city. Surrounded by overgrowth, he kept going, feeling through the pulse of power that now lay close ahead.

Looking over, Korin noticed Ádan's hand on his sword as Ádan watched all around. Ádan on alert was both reassuring and not.

"Are we still in the city?" Korin asked.

"No idea," Ádan answered softly. "I've never been down this road. I didn't even know it existed."

"You mean you've never been over in this part of cliffside?"

"No. I mean we went right by the zhi Yuesult estate. I've been to parties there. Lysander and I, we explored every inch of their gardens. I'm telling you, there wasn't a road."

Korin looked down at the worn stones, the divots and discolorations where weather had ground away the original work and it had been replaced. This road was old. Older than Ádan, at least. "Could you have just missed it?"

"No."

Which meant someone had been hiding it. With magic. "How easy is it to do something like that? This isn't my area of expertise," Korin admitted.

"You're talking big ritual magic. Which isn't my thing either."

They reached an estate—or what was left of one. The grounds had once been overgrown, but now everything was brown and brittle and dead. The outbuildings were rotting, their once beautiful domes now dotted with a handful of painted tiles that still clung to their place while the structure crumbled around them.

The road had curved back around to the cliffs. This manor had an incredible view and would have been an amazing place to live once. Now...

"Does someone really live here?" Korin asked.

"You're the one who led us here, Sunshine." Ádan drew his sword. "Let's see what we've found."

The great house looked only slightly more solid than the rest of the estate. Korin tested his foot on the steps, ready to jump back if anything crumbled. In silent accord, he and Ádan spread out, putting several feet of space between them so no part of the rotting floors had to bear both of their weight. Korin pushed open the front door.

Inside was nothing like Korin had expected. It was like he'd pushed his way into the past, when this manor had been something beautiful. Inside was lush and opulent and not a sign of decay.

And inside, at the base of the grand stairway, a man waited for them.

Neither old nor young, neither handsome nor ugly—this man was the epitome of nondescript. If Korin had passed him on the street, his eyes would have slid on by. There was nothing about this man to catch the attention.

Except for the sigil around his neck—a sigil that matched Korin's.

"How delightful," the man said, his voice as neutral and uninteresting as his appearance. "Guests. And me without so much as a pot of tea brewing."

"Forgive us for intruding," Korin said, his reflex for politeness covering his confusion.

"Not at all. I've been waiting for you to find me, Korin. It is Korin, yes?"

Korin nodded, unsurprised this stranger knew his name.

The man's eyes shifted to Ádan. "And who is this?"

"A friend," Korin answered. There was no reason for this wizard to know Ádan's name.

"How sweet." The man looked Ádan up and down, took in the sword that was still gripped tightly in Ádan's hand, and quite visibly dismissed Ádan, turning his attention back to Korin. "I'm so pleased you found me."

"You're the one—you've been hurting people. You've been…" Korin didn't even have a word for it, "unhealing them."

"It's true."

Korin was sickened by the fact the man didn't even try to deny it. "Why? How can you do something like that?"

"A test for you. Once which you've now passed. Well done."

"You hurt those people. Innocent people!"

The man flicked his hand, dismissing the complaint. "Meaningless rabble. Millions of them in the world, Korin, endlessly replacing themselves. They're not gifted like you and I. If you must use them to learn, that's one thing. But never mistake them for beings of any importance."

"Who *are* you?" Korin demanded.

It was Ádan who answered. "He's Archwizard Loukanos. Korin, meet the head of your order."

KORIN HAD NEVER IMAGINED... HE remembered Renée talking about his Archwizard in unrepeatable terms. He remembered rumors and flinches when people talked about wizards of the Staff. And most of all, he remembered Teriad's silence when questions about the rest of their order came up.

Korin had never imagined his Archwizard could be a man like this. "You're a monster."

Loukanos rolled his eyes. "Oh please, let's not be dramatic. I'm a wizard, the same as you. Practicing my magic, the same as you."

"No. Not the same at all. I help people."

Loukanos crossed arms, looking Korin up and down. "Help people. I see. Tell me, Korin, where do you come from? Who was your teacher?"

"I learned from Teriad."

"Ah yes, Teriad. Well, that does explain things."

Korin bristled at the snide tone. "Teriad was a good man."

"Teriad was..." Loukanos trailed off, a smile curling his lips. "It doesn't matter. We're not here to talk about Teriad. Except, perhaps, to say that Teriad was a wizard who decided to cripple himself. You have talent, Korin. That's been clear as I've followed your magic through this city. But if Teriad was your teacher, you don't understand half of what our magic is about."

"I understand enough."

"Do you?" His smile became cruel. "Fixing sprains and driving away coughs. You really think that's what our magic does? Is that truly all you aspire to?"

Korin couldn't imagine a level of desperation that would drive him to stay any longer in Loukanos's presence than he had to. "My aspirations are my own business. I'm not interested in anything you have to say."

"No?" The cruelty fell away so fast Korin had trouble remembering he'd seen it. Loukanos's expression was back to bland, unremarkable. "I've seen your work, Korin. You have skill and you have power. Are you going to look me in the eye and tell me you've never wondered if there isn't more to reach for? More that your magic can do?"

Korin couldn't hold back the shudder at having his thoughts spoken out loud by a man like this. What did it even mean that someone like Loukanos understood?

"Ah yes," Loukanos said, "I see you have thought about that. Do you even understand your potential? Korin, please, listen to me. Don't waste your life—your future—wearing the same bindings Teriad imposed on himself."

"Come on, Korin." Ádan's voice was hard. "You don't need to talk to him. We don't need to stay."

"Perhaps not, but consider," Loukanos said, "I don't care to be bored. If you're not here for me to teach—if you leave me with nothing to occupy my time—I'll have nothing better to do than to continue as I have been. Your little flock you're building—how long will they worship you if their ills and injuries keep coming back?"

Korin had never felt so helpless. Loukanos's threat—what could Korin even do to stop him?

Ádan's hand on his shoulder reminded him he could move. "Don't hurt any more people," Korin said, hearing the weakness in his own voice. Then he turned and walked out, slamming the door behind him.

KORIN HELD his peace until they were back out onto the road. His entire body was a tense ball of fear and anger. His throat was so tight, he could barely speak. He couldn't manage it at all until they were well away from the mansion.

Ádan, too, was quiet. Which was oddly infuriating. "Did you know?" Korin finally demanded.

"Know what?" Ádan asked. He sounded evasive. Or maybe Korin was imagining that because he expected it. Not that Ádan didn't have a history of keeping secrets.

"About Loukanos."

"I didn't know he was here in Triome," Ádan said. Which wasn't exactly an answer to the question Korin had asked.

"Did you know he was a monster?"

Ádan sighed. But he answered straight on. "Yes. I knew. Everyone knows. Renée told you as much, but you didn't want to listen."

"So this is my fault?"

"No!" Ádan stopped, grabbing Korin's hand and forcing Korin to stop too, to face him. "None of this is your fault. Don't think for a minute anything that man does reflects on you."

"He's hurting people because of me. He's going after people I've helped just to get my attention. And you heard him. He isn't going to stop. More people are going to get hurt because of me."

"Because of *him*," Ádan insisted in a cold voice. "He's spent his whole life hurting people. You're not responsible for his actions."

"But I am responsible for those people."

Ádan squeezed Korin's hands so tight it was almost painful. "Promise me you're not thinking of doing what he wants—of going back to—"

"No." Korin pulled free. He knew Ádan was trying to help, but Korin didn't want comfort right now. He didn't want empty reassurance. "I would never work with someone like that. I don't want to learn anything he would want to teach me."

So much to learn, the knife's voice whispered.

"No," Korin repeated. To her. To Ádan. To the universe. "No, that's not who I want to be. That can't be…" He turned away, burning with anger and guilt and helplessness.

Ádan put a hand on his shoulder. "What can I do?"

"Nothing." What could either of them do? Who had the power to fight an Archwizard? "Take me home." The words came out soft, pleading.

They returned to Marta's and retreated to Korin's room. Exhausted and dejected, Korin didn't have the energy to do much more than lie wrapped in Ádan's embrace. Eventually, he slept.

16

*K*ORIN WASN'T SURPRISED to wake alone, and today, he wasn't disappointed either. Clarity had come to him in the night, and he knew what he needed to do.

Ádan wouldn't like it. Korin wasn't sure he liked it himself, but he needed a way to stop Loukanos from hurting people, and Korin didn't have the power or authority to do that. For good or ill, he knew the person who did.

It was strange how comfortable he was getting just walking into the palace. Or how easy it was. This was not something he ever would have imagined imagined as part of his life.

He climbed to the garden. Sheluna was there, at the center of things, as she had been before. An Archwizard at the height of her power, as beautiful as she was dangerous. Samir wasn't here this morning. Just her and her tiger and the assortment of Wing wizards that always seemed to be milling about. Korin walked straight up to her. "Did you know Loukanos was in the city?" he asked without preamble.

Sheluna waved her fingers and the sounds of the garden disappeared. She and Korin were alone together in a bubble of privacy. It was an impressive display of magic, all the more so for the effortless way she'd done it. "Loukanos? I had my suspicions, but he has yet to reveal himself to me. We're not on what you would call friendly terms."

"Well he's here. And he's hurting people."

"Ah." One word. Full of understanding. "He's the wizard you've been chasing."

"He's been chasing me. That's why he's doing it, to get my attention. He..." Talking about it, saying the words out loud, made Korin's resolution crumble and he was left with the despair of yesterday. "I can't stop him. More people will get hurt. Because of me."

Ádan would have argued with those words, and Korin understood what he was saying, but the truth was, if Korin wasn't here, none of those people would be in danger.

Sheluna nodded. "I know how he likes to work."

"How can you allow it?" It was maybe not the most politic question, but Korin couldn't stop himself. "How can you know and still let it happen?"

Sheluna sighed, an exhausted sound. "The laws are what they are for a reason, but sometimes they allow people like Loukanos to escape consequences. Archwizards are forbidden to act against each other without the full backing of the council. And the council is... uninterested in more conflict now the war in Ulek has ended."

Korin's entire body tensed. "So you're saying there's nothing anyone can do."

"I'm saying at the moment, while he is Archwizard of the Staff, there is nothing *I* can do."

Korin caught the emphasis, understood what she was implying. "What can I do? He's an Archwizard."

"And you are a young man with both talent and passion." Sheluna leaned forward. "Do you know that Teriad once challenged Loukanos? They fought. Teriad lost, of course. But Teriad, for all his convictions, was never the most powerful wizard. He didn't have a chance against Loukanos. Which is probably why Loukanos let him live."

Korin was shocked. He couldn't imagine Teriad fighting anyone. Much less Teriad challenging an Archwizard. Teriad, who'd kept them isolated and as far away from politics as possible —that Teriad had once tried to take over the order?

"Here's what I think," Sheluna continued. "Teriad still believed someone different should be leading the Staff. Teriad still wanted to see the end of Loukanos—of all the horrible things that he's led the Staff to do. And then Teriad found you.

"I've done my homework, Korin. You healed people in Ulek. You've healed people here. You have power like Teriad never dreamed of. I believe Teriad saw that as clearly as I did. I believe Teriad had plans for you. He couldn't challenge Loukanos…but perhaps you can."

Korin knew he was gifted. Korin knew he was good at the magic he did. But what Sheluna was suggesting… "I'm not *that* good."

"Not yet," Sheluna agreed. "But you could be. With the right teacher."

Korin understood what she was offering. And he understood what she was asking for in return.

Korin wanted no part in wizard politics. Even in the best world, he wasn't interested in the games, in the attention, in any work other than the hands-on helping that he knew best. And this wasn't the best world. Korin's relationship with Ádan complicated things. The knife complicated things. How much actual scrutiny could Korin afford without betraying his friends? Without someone looking a little too close at Ádan?

But someone had to stop Loukanos. And it didn't seem as though anyone else was going to step forward to volunteer.

There was, in the end, only one answer Korin could give.

. . .

Wrapped in shadows, Ádan stood outside the decaying mansion, gathering his courage.

He'd slipped out before Korin awoke, as he often did. Today, he felt particularly guilty, knowing what Korin would say if he knew where Ádan was. Ádan would absolutely have rather lounged in bed, had breakfast together, and spent the day without a care in the world. Add that to the list of things Ádan could wish for but wasn't likely to get any time soon.

It was hard not to feel powerless. He'd been given an impossible task by Derian, and then sent away so he could do nothing but watch from a distance as Derian was destroyed by people who hated him. If that same thing happened to Korin, if Loukanos hurt Korin, or worse… Ádan couldn't, *wouldn't* let that happen.

What Ádan had was an idea. A terrible idea. A dangerous idea. No one would approve of this idea. Not Nikki or V; not Korin, not Lysander.

What Loukanos presented was an opportunity. Someone who understood the magic Ádan needed to understand. Someone who might understand it even better than Korin. Hadn't V himself said it? That they needed to learn about the magic themselves?

More importantly, this could keep Korin free and keep Korin safe. Ádan hadn't been able to help Derian, but this, Ádan could do.

Truly, what choice did he have? As much as Ádan might try to will better options into existence, the fact was he and V and Nikki were lost. The line between their current situation and absolute failure was so thin as to be almost invisible. It was going to take an act of desperation to save them.

Ádan crept forward, up the steps. The door was still unlocked. Ádan pushed it open, every sense alert for danger.

The smell inside was awful, but also familiar. Ulek had smelled like this in the end. Blood and rot, salt and cloying sweet and stomach-churning sour. It was the scent of death, of decay, of bodies corrupted. It was the scent of *wrong*.

Loukanos had relocated to a tall chair near the window; a book sat open in his lap. He looked boring, small. An almost perfect camouflage. He looked up at Ádan's entrance. "Oh how tedious," he muttered. "The friend."

"My name is Ádan."

"Ádan," Loukanos repeated in a bored tone. "Did you come back for a reason? To toss around threats, perhaps? To tell me to stay away from Korin?"

He sighed, closing the book and setting it aside. "I suppose as long as you're here, I might as well make use of you. How shall I send you back to Korin? Some broken bones? Something more contagious, perhaps?" He stood, and Ádan felt the magic wrapping around his limbs to hold him still.

Ádan pushed back. One of the first things any Knight learned was how to fight wizards—how to keep yourself safe from their magic. Conviction mattered more than raw power—Ádan's will demanding that his body was his own, that no one else held power over it. He slid free of Loukanos's influence and took a step forward.

Loukanos raised an eyebrow. After only the briefest pause, he said, "No sigil and no cross, so you're either a wizard breaking the law or…"

"Yes," Ádan confirmed. "The or."

Loukanos sat perfectly still as he thought. He didn't fidget, or act at all uncomfortable with the silence. He was a man in perfect control. "And how is it," he asked after a few very long moments, "that you aren't as dead as the rest of your compatriots?"

"I ran," Ádan answered flatly, without hesitation. "I saw what was coming. I saw there wasn't any hope. So I got out."

This was the first step of a dangerous dance. Ádan had been trained to lie, and to lie well, but Loukanos was like no one else Ádan had ever tried to mislead. He knew bodies, just like Korin, would be watching for the slightest flutter of pulse or temperature or twitch—the barest sign that Ádan let slip.

Ádan let that thought in, let it break against his mind, then released it. He couldn't afford the worry. He had to focus on believing his own story.

Loukanos, for now at least, wasn't calling him a liar. "So you escape the disaster in Ulek and you come to Triome, where you've hid in plain sight among the dissolute nobles and made friends with little Korin. And now—behind Korin's back—you come to me. And I wonder why."

"I find myself in need of a new occupation."

"I'm not looking to take on an apprentice."

"You wanted to teach Korin."

"Korin is special. And Korin already belongs to me." Loukanos looked up and down Ádan, gave a dismissive sniff. "You're too old to learn a brand new discipline with any facility. And that's assuming you can unlearn whatever broken techniques your masters drilled into you. Which is all presuming I had any interest in you in the first place."

Ádan had been trained as a spy and a manipulator, and the bread and butter of both those skills was the ability to read people. Loukanos was playing hard to get, but the fact they were still talking at all meant Loukanos wasn't as disinterested as he claimed.

What did Loukanos want? What could Ádan offer?

Why was Loukanos even here? Was it just about Korin? Or was Loukanos in Triome looking for other things?

Derian had been suspicious of all the wizards who made war against Ulek. The Darkivels had their own vendetta, but everyone else, Derian had wondered how much they sensed the knife. How much they sensed that power lurking. Now Loukanos was in Triome, where the knights had come from. Where the knife had returned. Was that a coincidence? Could it be?

If not, that was Ádan's bait. And the most dangerous game Ádan could play. "You're here looking for Derian's treasure, aren't you?"

Not a twitch from Loukanos, no sign to betray whether Ádan

had hit a nerve. But Ádan believed he had, all the same. "What treasure would that be?" Loukanos asked, his bored tone a little less convincing than before.

"I don't know. But there was something. Something he kept hidden. Something with power."

"What sort of power?" Loukanos asked, his tone too careful.

Got you. Ádan shrugged. "Like I said, it was hidden. I never saw it. But everyone in the castle could feel it there. And no one found it after."

How much could Loukanos see? How much did he know? If Loukanos saw through Ádan, would Ádan have any warning at all?

"If there were a lost treasure, and *if* I were interested in finding it, wouldn't I be in Ulek, rather than here?"

"Lots of people were in Ulek." Ádan picked his words carefully, but made sure to speak them quickly, casually. As though he had nothing to hide. "Seems to me, if that thing were easy to find, someone would have found it. But everyone knows the knights kept secrets in lots of places. If a person were looking to find those secrets, Triome is as good a place to look as any."

The trick here was to look like he was trying to be shrewd, to make Loukanos think he was seeing through Ádan's attempt to be clever. "Maybe we're both here looking for the same thing. Maybe we can help each other." Ádan stopped there. Important to not offer too much, to not seem too eager.

"What is it you think my help will get you?" Loukanos asked.

Ádan tamped down his relief with the same rigor he'd tamped down his fear. "I want a new life. I want someone new to be so I don't have to hide anymore."

"There are hundreds of wizards who could teach you. Including your friend Korin. Why come to me?"

The answer was obvious, but Loukanos was going to make Ádan say it. He wanted it out there between them so there were no misunderstandings of their position. "Most wizards would turn me in the minute they found out what I was. Including Korin." A risky lie, but a necessary one. "You have a reputation for being... less interested in the rules."

Loukanos stared at Ádan, his eyes piercing deep to where Ádan feared the man might be seeing his very soul. Just how much could Loukanos see? How much could he read? Ádan had been near the knife. Had its power brushed off on him in some noticeable way? Was there anything giving him away? Some cue he didn't realize was easily visible to the crafty old wizard?

The silence stretched. Ádan fought the urge to fidget. He called on every bit of his training to keep his mind clear, his posture easy. It was all right for Loukanos to understand this was important to Ádan, but Ádan couldn't afford for the old man to see that he was desperate.

Finally, Loukanos spoke. Two soft words. "Very well."

Now Ádan allowed himself a deep breath, a relieved sigh. "You'll teach me?"

"For a while. We'll see where this goes." Loukanos reopened the book in his lap. "Come back tomorrow. I'm done with you now."

17

*W*ORKING WITH SHELUNA was a revelation.

Teriad had been a skilled wizard and an excellent teacher. Korin learned so much from him. But Teriad had lived by his own agenda, and had spent half his time telling Korin what he couldn't—or shouldn't—do.

Sheluna was brilliant. Sheluna was fearless. Sheluna's eyes lit up at any question Korin thought to ask, excited to share even the most trivial idea she had about magic. She never criticized Korin for anything he didn't know, and she seemed genuinely impressed by what he did.

Korin wasn't just impressed by what Sheluna knew. He was dazzled.

The school of the Crystal was so small, Korin had taken a number of classes from Archwizard Perrault directly, so it wasn't as though Sheluna was the first Archwizard Korin had studied with. Perrault had been brilliant—no question. When it came to questions of math and physics, of how things worked on a macro or micro scale, there was nothing Perrault didn't understand. But ask him about magic outside his chosen field, and Perrault would shrug and move on.

Teriad had been the same way. They were wizards of the Staff, he'd say to Korin. There was more than enough magic to perfect within their field. It was foolish to waste time on questions and techniques other wizards were better suited to.

Sheluna didn't think that way. Sheluna didn't discourage any train of thought or line of magic.

It didn't matter that she was of the Wing and Korin was of the Staff. She accepted neither the limitation nor the excuse. If Korin didn't understand because he lacked a background in what she was talking about, well then she expected him to learn. And fast.

Korin loved the struggle, and even more he loved the implied respect. She expected Korin to be able to keep up, and he couldn't imagine any greater compliment. For the first time in his life, Korin felt seriously challenged.

Korin's life settled into a glorious new pattern.

Mornings at the palace with Sheluna. Working, exploring, challenging each other. A great deal of that time they spent in Sheluna's suite—a cluster of rooms in a palace wing that, as far as Korin could tell, permanently belonged to the Darkivels. A lavish parlor had been converted into a wizard work area. Furniture had been shoved into corners. Rugs pulled up. The tiled floor was painted with symbols and circles, and every spare surface was piled with books, papers, and the assorted trinkets that seemed to fast accumulate around wizards who didn't live their lives on the road —small pretty rocks, vials of oils and other fluids, powders of various colors, little dolls, and dried flowers.

And because Sheluna was a Wing wizard, the room was filled with animals. Hamsters and mice and birds in cages, out of cages, alive, dissected, stuffed. Two cats who came and went freely through the open windows. A little dog that Sheluna had no claim to, but seemed utterly fascinated by Cír. It was a strange environment to work in, but Korin was getting used to it.

Lunch was at the palace on days when he and Sheluna were still deep in discussion of technique or theory. On days when she had other engagements, or when they'd reached a point where they both needed to go away and think, Korin returned to Marta's and sat in the kitchen chatting with Holli, Verania, and Lily as they prepared for the evening meal. There was always fresh rice and warm leftovers from the night before, and more often than not on these days, before Korin had finished with the savory food, Marta had come through to slip him a pastry.

Afternoons were more magic. Easy magic. Maintaining the enchantments around Marta's, providing healing to anyone who came to the guesthouse to ask for him. There'd been a steady stream these last few weeks, but Korin had been happy to see that, so far, none of them were repeat customers. For whatever reason, Loukanos had paused his harassment. Korin didn't believe that would last, but he could enjoy the quiet while he had it.

Some days it was quiet enough he visited Renée, to join her for dinner or help her with whatever project held her current attention. Other days, the line of people who needed him kept Korin busy until well after dark. At which point he'd drag himself into the kitchen, wheedle more food from whoever was cooking, and retreat to his room to practice and study the concepts Sheluna was shoving into his head as fast as Korin could learn them.

Tonight, Korin sat cross-legged on his bed, shirtless and still sweating in the humid night air. Not even a slight breeze moved through his open window. Spring was turning into summer, and the heat was suffocating.

Korin had spent the latter part of the morning with Sheluna in one of the palace gardens, talking magic under the baking sun. Korin had been ready to melt, even with his shirt unlaced halfway down his chest and his feet bare in the grass. Sheluna, in her heavy velvet robes, had been as comfortable as ever. When Korin had complained, she'd only looked at him, her red eyes glowing softly with amusement, and said, "Aren't you a wizard?"

And thus it became a challenge. A matter of pride for Korin to figure out exactly what Sheluna was doing without asking for help.

She'd answer any questions he brought to her—she never withheld any knowledge she possessed if Korin asked—but to do so would be an admission that he couldn't work out the problem on his own.

She wasn't changing the air around her. The Wing sanctuary in the palace had been cool, but that cool air didn't follow Sheluna around. Which meant not only did Sheluna have a different trick, but it was one that not all her fawning cadre of followers had mastered.

No, whatever she was doing, it was a change she had made to herself.

Changing his body, could Korin do it?

Healing was a matter of returning the body to its natural state, putting things back the way they wanted to be. That was what Teriad had taught Korin. Healing could be complicated, intricate work, but the magic was always moving through paths the body knew, matching a pattern that already existed.

More complicated, more dangerous, was creating a new pattern. Bodies were complicated, interdependent systems and the slightest error of imagination could kill. Which was why Teriad had insisted no responsible healer ever attempted transformations or alterations beyond a body's default state.

Sheluna was…more open minded on the subject.

"You're cheating yourself," Sheluna had said, just this morning. "If you limit healing only to returning the body to some theoretical neutral state, you're only going halfway."

"I'm giving them their own bodies back," Korin had argued. "You can't go around changing people into something they aren't. Especially if they didn't ask you to. Besides, it's dangerous."

"It's arbitrary," Sheluna countered. "An injury, fine, that's an easy line to draw. Leg wasn't broken before. Now it is. So you fix it. But what about someone who comes to you sick? A pneumonia that damaged their lungs. A cancer that's eaten away their skin.

You don't just erase the disease. You try to recreate a healthy body for them."

"That's still putting things back the way they were supposed to be. It's just those parts were hurt longer, so you have to reach back further."

Sheluna had been sprawled back against Cír as they sat in the grass, scratching his head while they talked. "What about old age? Why not call that a disease? Why not put those people back the way they were when they were twenty? It's just a matter of reaching back."

"Age is supposed to happen. It's natural."

"Ah, natural." Sheluna's eyes had pulsed bright, the way they did when she felt strongly about something. "That's Teriad talking. I know, because I had this same discussion with him. He never listened to me. But you, Korin, you think about things. So consider this."

She leaned forward, prompting a growl from the tiger as she stopped scratching, which Sheluna ignored. "Magic is something we're born with. It's as much a part of us as breathing. So how is it unnatural to use it? Maybe natural is another arbitrary line. It presumes nature is something we need to emulate, which is another discussion entirely.

"Wizards are hypocrites, Korin. Especially our two orders. You say age is natural, but what wizard have you ever known who aged naturally?"

"That's just because of what we are. It's the magic—"

Sheluna shook her head, disappointment clear on her face. "You know better. Or you would if you thought about it."

She wouldn't say any more. She really meant for him to think about it.

So Korin sat, eyes closed, hands on his knees, focused on his body, and thinking.

Until Ádan's voice from the window said, "Well now, this is a pretty sight."

18

*K*ORIN OPENED HIS eyes and couldn't hold back his smile at the sight of Ádan straddling the windowsill, watching Korin. Korin felt himself blush, as he always did when Ádan looked at him in that particularly appreciative way.

These last couple weeks had been strange and…well, not awkward, exactly—Korin hardly ever felt awkward when he was actually with Ádan—but there was a definite nervousness he felt the rest of the time.

Every morning at the palace, he felt a constant nervousness about running into Ádan, afraid of what he'd say if Ádan asked what he was doing there. Ádan had been clear about his dislike and mistrust of Sheluna—and Korin could certainly understand why he'd feel that way.

Korin wasn't going to lie to Ádan. If Ádan asked, Korin would tell him.

Ádan hadn't asked. Ádan hadn't been around the palace. Ádan hadn't been around much at all. When he did come by—evenings, like this, where he'd show up late and be gone again by morning—he'd been tired and quieter than usual, content to listen to Korin talk through whatever metaphysical puzzles or interesting healings were on his mind that night.

Korin wanted to ask, but this was delicate, dangerous ground. The most likely answer was Ádan was doing work for the knights, for the knife, and Korin had made clear he didn't want to be part of that.

When Korin had said that, he'd been hurt, still recovering from the shock of the knife and being kidnapped by the knife's worshippers. It had seemed like a reasonable line to draw. Only now was Korin realizing just how much of a wall that could put between them.

A wall Korin wasn't helping with his own secrets.

Ádan was still quiet, still sitting in the window, staring at Korin with an intensity that Korin didn't know how to interpret. "Ádan? Are you okay?"

"Never better than when I'm with you." Ádan swung his other leg inside. "What were you thinking about so seriously?"

"Magic." It was an evasive answer, but also a true one.

And it made Ádan smile. "When are you not thinking about magic?"

"When I'm thinking about you." The words felt incredibly daring, and Korin looked down, second-guessing them as soon as they came out of his mouth.

When he glanced back up, Ádan's smile had fallen away. Looking directly into Korin's eyes, he said, "I want you to know that you are the best thing in my life right now. And I will never not be thrilled that you're thinking about me."

Korin wasn't sure how to respond to that. Ádan being serious made his stomach twist—both from the words themselves and the fact that it wasn't what he expected.

If Ádan noticed his discomfort, he didn't say. Instead, he flopped down on the bed with easy familiarity and pulled Korin into his lap. "So talk to me about magic." The usual lightness had returned to his tone. "Tell me what idea's got you all deep and thinky today."

"I'm trying to figure out..." Korin had to stop and backtrack several times in his mind, to organize the problem in a way he could explain it from scratch. "I'm trying to figure out, what are the limits of healing? What are we doing, exactly? Why are some things okay and other things not?"

"Like what? Give me examples?"

That was one of the things Korin liked so much about Ádan, that he jumped into these conversations feet first, like it was the most natural thing in the world to be talking about. He never asked why Korin would be thinking about such things, or told him it was silly, or pointless...or wrong.

"Okay, so for example, if you break your leg, I heal you by putting the leg back to the way it was before it was broken."

Ádan nodded.

"But on the other hand, say you get old."

"As people do," Ádan said in a dry tone.

"Exactly. Why don't we heal age? What would that be other than just setting the body back...farther."

Ádan's fingers traced light trails back and forth across Korin's thighs as he considered. "You said yourself that it was harder to heal after the body had time to adjust. Healing old age would require reaching really far back, yes?"

"Yes. And it would be hard. But not impossible."

"Okay." Ádan fell thoughtfully silent.

Korin took the next step. "Then, if making someone younger is okay, why not other things? Why not taller, or stronger? Why not more?"

"I guess my first question would be, who are you arguing against? Who decided you can't do those things?"

That was a good question. Teriad was the first answer that came to mind, but Korin knew exactly what Ádan would say to that—that Teriad was dead. His next instinct was to say that it was just wrong and everyone knew it. But…right and wrong had to come from somewhere, yes? It certainly wasn't something defined by council law. Korin couldn't do these things to someone without their permission, but nowhere was there a strict listing of what magic wizards were or weren't allowed to do.

"I'll have to think about that."

"They're good questions," Ádan said. "I'll be interested to hear what answers you come up with."

"Yeah, so will I."

Ádan tucked Korin against him, stroking Korin's hair as he closed his eyes. "I don't know about you, Sunshine, but I'm beat. Do you mind if we just lie down for a bit?"

"Not at all." It was on the tip of Korin's tongue to ask what Ádan was doing that had him so exhausted. But…if it was something Ádan wanted Korin to know, surely he would tell him. So instead, he stretched out next to Ádan and they laid quietly together until Korin's own eyes started to flutter shut.

KORIN OPENED his eyes to pitch darkness. And cold. And silence.

Was this a dream? It had to be. No matter how real it felt, it couldn't be. Korin had gone to sleep in his room, in his bed, Ádan's arms wrapped around him.

So this *was* a dream, no matter that Korin vividly felt the cold air moving over his skin, or that he could hear the rough echo of his breath in the unnatural stillness.

Korin summoned a light—and froze. He knew where he was. He'd been here before. Once.

He was underground, in a cavern of cold stone. His light couldn't reach all the way to the ceiling, but Korin knew where the ceiling was. Just as he knew that above him was a walkway, a place where someone could stand and look down at the cavern floor where Korin knelt. If someone had been up there, they would have been able to see him on his knees.

Before the tree.

A dream, Korin reminded himself. He was asleep in his room, with Ádan beside him. This wasn't real.

The snake, moonlight-pale and thick as Korin's thigh slithered down from the high branches. **You avoid me. You deny me.**

"I never asked for you."

But you did. You asked for my help and I gave it.

"That was a mistake. You hurt that man. *We* hurt that man."

I am bound. I am imprisoned. I did all that I could do. If I were free...

"No." Korin got to his feet and backed away. "It was a mistake. I won't do it again. If that's what you want—"

What I want. The snake reared back, its tongue flicking out to taste the air. **What I want.** She sounded...confused. Maybe even lost.

Korin knew that feeling well enough. "What do you want?"

The snake dropped lower, wrapping herself around the lowest branch before reaching out to him, her head bobbing back and forth. Korin lifted his hand to meet her and her head brushed his wrist, slid around his arm and up until her head was before his face. She leaned in, and her tongue flicked against his nose, his lips. Her eyes, glittering pools of shadow, held his. He couldn't look away.

Korin jerked awake, felt Ádan's arms tighten around him, then release as soon as he started to struggle. Korin rolled out of bed, needing to stand, needing to breathe.

"Bad dreams again?" Ádan asked, blurry with sleep. He sat up, rubbing at his eyes.

He looked so tired. What was he doing to make him so tired? Korin almost asked, before better sense overrode his instinct to be concerned. Opening the floor to questions right now was a bad idea. So instead, he said, "I'm sorry for waking you up."

"It's all right." Ádan stood up, grimaced as he stretched. "I should go, anyway. I didn't mean to fall asleep like that."

You needed it, Korin thought, but didn't say. "I'm glad you came by."

Ádan stepped into him, slid a finger under Korin's chin. "I like seeing you. I…" He took a deep breath, and his lips spread into a familiar, bright smile. "I'll see you again soon."

"Promise," Korin said.

Ádan leaned in and kissed him, soft and lingering. "Promise," he whispered against Korin's lips.

After he left, Korin lay back down. Feeling guilty for not asking questions, for the secrets he was keeping. Feeling worried. Feeling…

It had only lasted a moment, the connection between Korin and the knife. A moment no longer than a heartbeat where he'd fallen into her eyes and he'd felt…everything.

So much pain. So much loneliness. So much…fear? Yes, fear. The knife was afraid. Of what? Korin had no idea. But he'd felt it. He'd felt the depths of everything—the power. It had been overwhelming. It had been terrifying.

That hadn't been all. The pain had been the worst, but it hadn't been everything. Korin had felt something else. Just as strong, just as desperate.

Korin had felt love.

He didn't know what to think or how to respond. Or even if any of what she'd shared had answered the question of what the knife wanted.

All he knew was that the answers, if they existed at all, weren't going to be easy ones.

19

*Á*DAN EASED THE door open, lifting up on the handle at just the right spot so that it wouldn't creak. He slipped inside then closed it just as silently. His footsteps were whispers across the wood floor, quiet as a ghost.

It didn't matter. "Ádan!" Loukanos's voice from upstairs. Summoning him.

Ádan couldn't hide from Loukanos, not with magic or without. This was one of the many truths Ádan had learned in his weeks of study with the Archwizard. It was one of the least terrifying. If Ádan had it to do over again, knowing what he now knew, he would never have agreed to this devil's bargain.

Except that if Ádan weren't here, Loukanos might be focusing all his malevolent power and brilliance on Korin. And that was unacceptable. Ádan would pay whatever cost was necessary to keep that from happening.

Loukanos was in his study. Ádan still couldn't enter the room without gagging. The smells of mold, and blood, and rot were thick. Loukanos had a body on the table before him. It was breathing, Ádan noted, but judging by its swollen, decayed state, it was no longer alive.

"Did you have a nice nap?" Loukanos asked without looking up from where his hands were sunk wrist-deep into the body's chest cavity.

Loukanos didn't sleep. That was one of the things Ádan wished he had known before. He also didn't seem to eat. Ádan was pretty sure Loukanos survived on energy he pulled out of the bodies both living and dead he came into contact with. However Loukanos was sustaining himself, he was derisive of Ádan's need for both sleep and sustenance, and the interruptions they demanded.

For all Loukanos had sneered at Ádan's potential as an apprentice, he was awfully annoyed at the times when he didn't have Ádan here to assist.

"Come look at this," Loukanos said, ignoring the fact Ádan hadn't answered his last question. "Tell me what you see."

Ádan came closer. Lucky that he'd never been squeamish, even before he'd started training with the Knights. If Ádan had revealed any discomfort around the bodies Loukanos worked with, it would have been a weakness Loukanos would have delighted in using against him.

But even knowing that, Ádan couldn't stop himself from flinching back as soon as he got a good, close look.

"Aha," Loukanos said. "You recognize it."

Not alive—couldn't be alive—but the body was breathing and Ádan saw the tiny pulsing movements at its jaw that showed a heart was beating. Ádan had seen this trick before, with Loukanos recreating functions in the body to test various ideas. Ádan had gotten used to it.

This body was rotting, falling apart, its skin bloated and discolored and, in places, gone, to the point Ádan couldn't suss out any part of the body's identity, but that wasn't what had made Ádan pull back either.

More than decay. Black lines under the skin. Patches growing out from open sores. A dark, spreading mold that had rippled as Ádan got close. "The blight."

"Is that what you call it? Excellent. I expected you'd be familiar with it."

This was dangerous ground. Ádan knew all sorts of things about the blight. Some things any knight would have observed. Some things he knew because of his training, his tie to the knife. And some things he knew because Korin had figured them out. He'd have to guard every word.

While some of his thoughts were organizing and arranging the correct story to tell, others were taking note of the fact that Loukanos had his hands—his power—deep inside the blighted corpse. Ádan remembered how the blight had reached for Korin the first time he'd tried to heal it. The way it had responded to his magic, had seemed to draw strength, how he'd been in danger of being consumed. Loukanos was having none of those problems.

"Be careful," Ádan said as his truth construct solidified in his mind. "I've seen that spread into people. Corrupt them."

"And that's why you Knights should never have broken away from the Wizard Orders. You have absolutely no idea what you're doing."

This was the way to get information out of Loukanos. Not through questions. Loukanos hated questions. But if Ádan was patient, gave careful prompts—especially opportunities to insult other people's facility with magic—Loukanos would talk plenty.

Ádan reached his hand carefully forward, ready to pull back if the blight reacted to him. "I saw Knights—towards the end of the war, a number of them—who were sick with this. It spread through them like a plague."

"It's not a plague," Loukanos said. He pulled his hands from the body and the heartbeat stilled. "Watch."

Moments after the heart stopped, the body ceased breathing as well. All the forced symptoms of life fell away. As they faded, so did the black lines and blighted patches.

"It loses interest once the host is truly dead," Loukanos muttered.

"Interest?" Ádan carefully controlled his voice, kept the alarm from it. "Are you saying there's intent—a mind controlling this?"

"There's power; that much is certain. Power that exists here as well as in Ulek."

Loukanos seemed to be in a talkative mood, so Ádan risked a, "I don't understand."

Loukanos picked up a towel to wipe his hands, then dropped the towel over the body and waved an idle hand. Both erupted into instant, intense flames and burned away like they were made of flash paper. "Do you know why bread molds?"

"Because it gets old?" Ádan was genuinely confused by the change of subject.

"Yes, but how does the mold happen? How does it spread from bread to bread, everywhere? Over and over, the same result?"

Ádan had honestly never thought about it, but two weeks with Loukanos had honed his mental reflexes to a razor edge. The answer came without him having to think. "Because it's in the air, not the bread." Ádan paused. "Are you comparing the blight to mold?"

"In a sense." Loukanos gestured for Ádan to follow, led them out of the workshop. "I first noticed it in Ulek, that given the right environment, this blight would sprout. And then your dying knights somehow gave it a perfect environment. Now, it's here in Triome. It makes me curious."

Down the stairs, to the first floor library. "It's time to make yourself useful. You know the signs and symptoms; that's good. I want to know where else the blight has put in an appearance. Who else in the world has seen it."

"You want me to research?"

"Yes, but not here. I can read my own books perfectly well. There's a better library in the city."

The School of the Balance. "You don't want the other wizards to see you."

Loukanos gave a thin smile. "I simply have no interest in

exchanging meaningless small talk with my colleagues. So you'll go in my stead. You were a student. They'll let you in."

"It's a big library. It's going to take me a while to go through it."

"Not too long, I hope. You'd hate for me to get bored and have to seek out…other entertainments."

By which he meant Korin. "I understand."

"I hope you do. Now get out. Go find answers for me."

20

*I*T WAS LATE. Korin had been out all day, and into the night, but he was so exuberantly happy it was hard not to skip on his way home to Marta's.

Today he'd figured it out. Today, he'd figured a lot of things out.

The whole day had been spent with Sheluna and Samir. Samir, it turned out, was Sheluna's apprentice, and every bit as bright as one would expect her apprentice to be. They'd been so deeply immersed in talk about theory and in actual experimentation that they hadn't broken up for lunch, for the afternoon, for dinner. Sheluna had even blown off a scheduled meeting with the Archwizard of the Balance in order to keep working. Because she, too, was excited as Korin came closer and closer to internalizing and truly understanding everything she'd been talking about.

Other things Korin now understood—why Wing wizards kept all those animals around. Staff wizards might know the human and firstborn bodies like no others, but Korin now had to wonder why they stopped there. Comparisons, variations—that was the key.

For example, this problem Korin had been working on—how to stay cool in the heat using magic. Sheluna's challenge that she'd refused to just give him the answer to. Korin had spent day after day in meditation, in deep thought, tracing the lines and pathways of his body to try to figure out what might make things better.

And then today, he'd seen the answer. Not by looking at himself. But when Samir had brought his own current project for Sheluna to critique—a project that involves three little desert creatures Korin had never seen before. And Korin, out of curiosity, had looked at them with the same close study as he'd give to a patient brought before him.

These were creatures adapted to the heat, and Korin was able to see how they worked. Blood—that was the key. All three were different looking on the outside, but each of them had a part or all of their body with thin skin and a thick web of capillaries to move a lot of blood—blood that would cool quickly and efficiently before returning into the body.

All this worry Korin had been going through about ethics and unnatural changes, but this—this was so subtle, so easy—what had he been afraid of?

Sheluna had been excited when Korin had figured it out. And from there, the discussion had moved from *how does this work* to *how can we make it work even better* and thus the entire day had flown by before any of the three of them had noticed.

And now as he walked home, Korin was comfortable for the first time since he'd come to Triome. He wasn't too warm. In fact, he might even be a touch chilly with the sun gone and the evening breeze off the ocean.

And all the while Korin wondered—what else could he do?

The house was dark and quiet, but Korin had a key. He tiptoed in and crept his way up the stairs. Just as quietly, he eased open his own door. Only after he'd slipped inside and closed it just as softly did he realize that the people in other rooms weren't the only sleepers he was trying not to disturb.

Ádan was asleep in his bed, all curled up around Korin's pillow. It was a sign of just how exhausted Ádan must be that he was still asleep. Korin had found Ádan to be an extremely light sleeper, sensitive to every twitch or uneven breath Korin made when they were sleeping together. Now, he hadn't even stirred.

What *was* Ádan doing that had him so completely wiped out? It only seemed to be getting worse.

He must have made some noise because Ádan's eyes flew open. A sleepy smile spread across his face. "Hey, Sunshine."

And there it was—the look in Ádan's eyes. Warmth and affection and relaxed, easy happiness. Korin would never get tired of that look. He wanted to gift those feelings back to Ádan until Ádan forgot everything else.

So he sat down on the bed, ran a hand lightly down Ádan's arm, and said, "I've been learning some new tricks. Want to see?"

"SEE WHAT?" Ádan sat up, bleary-eyed, and looked at the night sky, visible through the window. "You were out late."

That wasn't the direction Korin wanted the conversation to go at all. He ran his hands up Ádan's chest, caught his lips in a kiss.

Ádan's hands came up, rested lightly on either side of Korin's head as Ádan pressed forward into the kiss. "Korin," he whispered. It sounded almost like a plea. He took a deep breath, his shoulders and chest moving against Korin's, then pulled back. He looked more awake now, wearing a familiar grin. "New tricks?"

Korin nodded. "Lie down." He felt himself blushing as he added, "Without your clothes."

Ádan raised an eyebrow in inquiry, but he did as he was asked. Korin watched—how could he not?—as Ádan peeled away his layers of fine clothing to reveal the lean, muscular body beneath. Fully naked, he stretched out on his back, arms over his head, obviously posing. "Like this?"

Distracted by the sight, it took Korin two tries to answer, "Turn over."

Ádan rolled onto his stomach and settled comfortably with his head on his folded arms. It occurred to Korin that at no point in this had Ádan asked Korin what he would be doing. He'd accepted the instructions he'd been given and now waited to see what Korin had in mind.

Ádan trusted him.

How was Korin living up to that trust? By pushing Ádan away. By refusing to be part of Ádan's life. Korin had drawn a line between Ádan the man and Ádan the knight, and now, when Ádan was clearly struggling, what could Korin offer other than a few moments of escape? This wasn't support. This wasn't partnership.

But this also wasn't the time to worry about it. Not when Ádan was tired—and naked—and so obviously needed Korin to just take care of him. Which Korin could do, in potentially very interesting ways.

Korin straddled Ádan, resting his weight on Ádan's thighs. "Is this all right?"

"Absolutely," Ádan murmured, eyes closed.

Korin ran his hands up Ádan's back. A light touch at first, with no magic. His fingers traced the lines of Ádan's muscles, felt the smooth expanse beneath him, watched the twitching movements under Ádan's dark skin. So much tension. Everywhere Korin touched, he met resistance. Ádan was tight.

Well that, Korin could definitely fix. He pressed, gentle, but firm. Turning his explorations into a massage.

Korin didn't need magic for this. He knew the muscles, the body, well enough to find all the places where tension settled and work them with his fingers and the heel of his hand. Ádan gave a happy groan as Korin pressed into his shoulders, kneading spots that felt like they'd been held too tight for far too long.

Rather than dig too deeply into the knots, Korin did send a few little threads of magic. Without magic, those pressure points could hurt before they released, and Korin didn't want Ádan to feel anything but relaxed. He worked down Ádan's sides, along his spine, to the small of his back.

"You are amazing. Have I told you that lately?" Ádan's murmur was practically a purr.

Korin's cheeks heated. A mix of pleasure at the compliment and continued guilt over the separation he was forcing Ádan to maintain. He didn't know what to say, so he focused on Ádan's body. Which was now completely relaxed. Time to change tactics.

Once again, Korin ran his hands lightly up and down Ádan's back. This time, he closed his eyes and sunk into Ádan with his magic. After days of intense study of minute reactions both within and without his own body, Korin could now easily pick up the tiniest signals moving through Ádan's flesh. He watched the patterns, like tiny sparks, as Ádan's skin felt Korin's touch and reported those touches through Ádan's nervous system.

Korin pulled back his hands, focused his mind, and recreated those signals.

Ádan gave a happy sigh.

Korin smiled. Yes, this was going to be fun.

He kept that pattern going, the tracing touch of fingers stroking down Ádan's back, and leaned forward to stroke lightly across Ádan's shoulders.

Ádan twitched and his eyes flew open. He twisted his head around. Korin's eyes were still closed, but he was tuned in to Ádan's body so deeply it was like he could see. "Shh," he said. "It's all right. It's magic."

Ádan lay back down. "It felt like you'd suddenly grown more hands." As Korin resumed, Ádan groaned with pleasure. "Okay, I take it back. *Now* you're amazing."

Korin leaned down and kissed him right between his shoulder blades. "Want to see how many of these I can keep up?"

"Yes. Please."

Hands stroking down Ádan's back, across his shoulders, down his arms, up his thighs, through his hair, and Korin was starting to reach his limit. As he added each new touch, he tried to bundle them together in his mind, but it became a complicated web of sensation to keep track of and keep going. He didn't want to push too hard and accidentally flare too much power. That might hurt Ádan, which was utterly unacceptable.

With practice, though, Korin thought he could do better. Or maybe Sheluna would have ideas for a different way to think about it, to manage—

Korin blushed again, happy Ádan wasn't watching him. Was he actually thinking about talking to Sheluna about the theory of how to better use magic for sex?

And then, a second thought, was there any way to make this sound more scholarly? Because she probably would have ideas.

Tomorrow's problem. Right now, what mattered was Ádan, who was undeniably enjoying this. "Roll over," Korin said.

Ádan languidly obeyed. He stretched out on his back, with a relaxed smile, his eyes half-closed, and a look of bliss on his face.

Time to up the game. Korin leaned down and circled his tongue around first one nipple, then the other. Ádan's hand reflexively came up to grip the back of Korin's head. Encouraging. Korin repeated the act, this time tracing it with magic so the sensations continued as he pulled away.

He moved lower, rubbing his cheek lightly across Ádan's stomach. That earned him another groan of pleasure. So Korin kept that going as well.

Leaving him just enough focus for one more loop of sensation, which Korin created by licking his lips and sliding his mouth over and down Ádan's straining cock.

Korin sat up to admire his handiwork. Ádan's eyes were completely closed. His hands were clenched in Korin's sheets, his body arched up into the sensations Korin's magic was creating. It was amazing to watch, and Korin had done this.

Korin wrapped his hand where his mouth had been, and stroked in time with the magic. He watched Ádan squirm, heard him sigh, watched the shudder of pleasure run through him as he came.

Korin released the magic and lay down next to Ádan. With his eyes still closed, Ádan said, "I can't move. I think I've melted."

"That was pretty much my goal." Korin kissed him, a feather-light brush across Ádan's lips.

Ádan mumbled, already almost back asleep. The only word Korin could make out was, "Perfect."

Which gave Korin another stab of guilt.

All these new tricks he was learning from Sheluna—what if Korin used them to help Ádan?

But that would be helping the knights.

But Ádan *was* the knights. And Varajas. And even Nikki.

The line between good and evil had been easier when the knights had been a faceless enemy, a monolith of people doing horrible things. Now the most horrible person in view was a wizard who wore the same sigil as Korin and everything was more complicated than he'd ever imagined.

Unable to resolve his spiraling thoughts, Korin finally fell asleep.

ÁDAN HAD TRAINED HIMSELF, years ago, to wake quietly from nightmares. It was an important skill when you weren't supposed to be someone who should be having nightmares at all. Now it meant Korin lay undisturbed, curled up and asleep with his back against Ádan, even after Ádan had come quite suddenly awake.

Another dream of Derian, hanging, and the haunted Ulek he had left behind. In his dream, the crows had circled around Ádan, pecking at him, but that hadn't been the part that had threatened to set him screaming.

Derian, faceless and decaying despite the magic that had been put on him, had raised a hand, pointed an accusing finger at Ádan. Ádan had backed away, turning to run, and behind him...

Behind him, in the cloud of crows, stood Korin. His face, too, had been destroyed by the scavengers. His body, too, was rotting.

He pointed the same finger at Ádan. This was Ádan's fault. Ádan's doing.

With gentle care, Ádan extricated himself from the bed and began, silently, to dress. He'd needed this, needed to see Korin and touch Korin, but he'd been away too long.

It got harder and harder to maintain his resolve to return to Loukanos, to make the active choice to return to that horror. Korin was the reminder. Seeing him helped Ádan keep strong.

This was the duty he'd been handed by Derian. This was what Derian had died for. The knife was an evil. Dangerous enough on its own, but in the hands of someone like Loukanos it would cause so much suffering, so much pain, so much death.

Derian had talked in grand visions and sweeping altruism. They were working to keep the world safe. To protect people who couldn't protect themselves. Ádan understood and agreed with those goals, but they were so abstract. Korin—he was Ádan's focal point. Ádan couldn't stay strong for the world, but he could stay strong for Korin.

Keeping Korin safe from Loukanos, from the knife, from everything—that was the one right thing Ádan had left. Making certain that nightmare never came true.

Ádan dropped a phantom kiss on Korin's forehead, light enough there was no chance of Korin waking. With that, he slipped silently out of the room.

21

KORIN AWOKE EARLY and alone. He was used to that. Much as he wished Ádan would stay longer, he didn't want to make demands.

Sheluna was in her workspace, at her cluttered desk, writing. Cír was sprawled at her feet, twisted into a pose that only a cat could find comfortable, with his back feet pointed one way and his front feet up in the air, pointed the opposite. His tail twitched when Korin came into the room, but the tiger had gotten used to Korin, and didn't even bother to open his eyes.

Sheluna, likewise, didn't look up, until Korin said, "What if everything I've ever been taught about magic is wrong?"

That made her smile, but she kept writing, holding up a finger for Korin to wait. Only after she got to the end of the page did she set down the pen and turn her chair to face him. "What brought this on?"

"Everything. All the things you've been saying. Every new thing I've tried. These experiments you and I have done—why haven't I been studying magic like this all my life?"

Sheluna's eyes pulsed a soft red glow of pleasure. "Now you're starting to see. There are entire worlds outside the rules you've been taught."

Korin sat down next to Cír, who tilted his head back and looked at Korin through narrowed eyes—an imperious demand for chin scritches. Which Korin obeyed. "Then why have the rules at all?"

"Because magic is dangerous," Sheluna answered in a matter-of-fact tone. "And because there are people who would abuse it. Wizards who would be a danger to themselves and to the people around them without the rules. But then there are the brilliant, gifted few—like you, Korin—who can transcend, for whom the rules are unnecessary restriction."

Not just like him. "Like you too."

"Well of course." Sheluna waved his statement away like it was a given. "I'm an Archwizard. The rules for us are different."

This whole direction of thinking made Korin uncomfortable, and he wasn't entirely sure why. "The laws—the rules, are there to protect people. It's one thing to say that you and I are different, but if we start ignoring some of them, what's to stop us from ignoring all of them?"

"You mean what's to stop you from becoming Loukanos?"

Korin hadn't been thinking that, except…yes, yes he had. "It seems like a poor system if the rules are only rules for some people."

"Whereever did you get the sense this was a good system?" She was being flippant. Korin waited for the real answer. After a long moment, she continued. "Power is a construct. Society is a construct. The world is a constant struggle between the people who want to hoard the power and use it for their own selfish ends versus the people who want to spread the power to help the most people. Every system was made by people, people who were doing their best, but who couldn't see every single edge case."

Cír nudged Korin's hand and gave a delicate—but still startling

—nip. Korin had stopped petting as he was listening. He quickly resumed.

Sheluna smiled at the exchange, but her eyes remained serious. "I'm the Archwizard of the Wing. I'm also a Darkivel. If I wanted to be like Loukanos, there are very few people who could stop me. So what you're asking, the real answer is, *you*. You are the one who stops yourself from becoming like him. Or doesn't."

None of these were comforting answers, especially since Korin couldn't find a way to argue with them. He couldn't keep from thinking about the old man, the hurt Korin had caused him by trying to work with the knife. That had been a huge failure of judgement. "How do I know? How do I trust that I'm doing the right thing? That I'm not breaking the rules selfishly? That I'm not going to hurt people?"

"You *are* going to hurt people. That's life. None of us get through it without...mistakes." Her voice held an edge of wistfulness, of sadness. "But you learn from those mistakes and resolve to minimize the harm you cause.

"Confidence, Korin. That's your real lesson. Trust in yourself. Not because of what I would say, or what Teriad would say, but because you're listening to the voice at the core of you. Do you think you can do that?"

He wanted to ask more questions, to argue that he didn't know how to find that voice, how to trust that voice. But in the spirit of what she was saying, he made himself say, "I'm ready to try."

Sheluna nodded. "Good. What, then, shall we focus on today?"

Korin was ready for this question. "Magical effects. Maintaining them—a number of them—and how to weave them into a larger pattern so I can handle more of them at once."

Sheluna's eyes grew thoughtful and their morning work began.

· · ·

AFTER HOURS of brainstorming and experiments and theory, Korin was mentally exhausted and no further along than he had been before, but he felt energized all the same. He and Sheluna had done good work and tomorrow they'd do more and he was absolutely confident they'd find a way to approach this problem and solve it.

Sheluna had to stop for a lunch engagement—something political that Korin had no interest in—so Korin contemplated heading down to town to try to catch Renée for food and possibly more talk of magic theory. But as he was crossing through the gardens, he was intercepted.

Korin recognized Prince Lysander from the parade the day Ádan had returned. From a distance, he'd been dazzling. Close up, he was even more impressive. Taller than Korin had realized—tall even for one of the firstborn, with chiseled features and cheekbones that could cut glass.

What surprised Korin was that Lysander recognized him. "Korin, right?"

Korin nodded cautiously.

Lysander seemed to notice he was making Korin nervous. He took a step back, raised his empty hands. "It's all right. I'm not here to cause you any trouble. I was just..." He lowered his voice, leaned in just a little. "Have you seen Ádan recently?"

"I saw him—" Korin stopped himself before he finished with *last night*. He didn't know what Lysander knew about Ádan, about Ádan and Korin, or what might get Ádan into trouble. "I've seen him," Korin corrected.

"Oh good," Lysander said with visible relief. "I was getting worried. It's been weeks since he's been around. But he told me about you, that you were a friend, and I was hoping you knew where he'd been."

Ádan had talked about him to Lysander. That gave Korin a happy burst of warmth. Enough that it almost distracted him from the rest of what Lysander had said. "Weeks? That long since you've seen him?"

Lysander shrugged. "I know he has…duties. Concerns that occupy his time right now. I just wanted to make sure he was all right."

The idle concern Korin had been feeling about Ádan's exhaustion, his distractedness, started to grow louder. "I'll tell him you asked."

So it wasn't purely luck Ádan hadn't caught Korin here at the palace. Ádan hadn't been coming to the palace. Which made Korin wonder…what *was* Ádan doing with his time?

So instead of heading towards Renée's, Korin pointed himself towards a different part of the city. Towards the other place he was likely to find people who might know where to find Ádan.

The Sandy Fox did a brisk business at lunch. It was packed full, loud and hot, even with its open, breezy walls. Ádan wasn't here—that had been too much to hope for—but someone else Korin recognized. A redhead in muted colors at a tiny corner table all alone.

Nikki and Korin weren't exactly friends. True, Nikki had helped save Korin's life, but before that, he had lied to Korin and thrown rocks at his head to try to keep Korin away from Ádan. His goal had been to protect the knights' secrets; he didn't trust wizards. Korin was gaining a better understanding of that, but he wasn't entirely comfortable around Nikki yet.

Today, though, he hoped they could be allies. Korin sat down across from Nikki, who looked up from his rice bowl and lifted his eyebrows. "Yes?"

"I'm looking for Ádan."

Nikki rolled his eyes. "You'd know better than I would. At least, I can only assume it's your pretty little ass that's kept him away."

Korin's unease grew another couple notches. "How long since you last saw him?"

"A few weeks. Why?" Nikki set his spoon down, really focused on Korin for the first time since Korin had joined the table. "Haven't you seen him?"

"Here and there. Every few nights, but even then, not for long."

"Lysander—" Nikki began.

Korin cut him off. "Hasn't seen him at all."

Nikki considered for a moment. "It isn't like Ádan to shirk his duties."

"What duties? You aren't—"

"Not here." Nikki stood and grabbed Korin by the sleeve. "Come on. We need to talk."

THIS WAS the second time Korin had been in the Knight's safehouse, the underground mansion both hidden and protected by magic. Like last time, he was too distracted to appreciate its grandeur.

Nikki led Korin to a room he hadn't seen before—a training room, full of dulled weapons and grass-filled mats where a shirtless Varajas was dueling an imaginary foe. By the amount of sweat he'd worked up, he'd been at this a while. Nikki dragged Korin over to the mat and said, "We've got a problem."

Varajas didn't miss a step, stabbing and twirling away from an anticipated counter-strike. "Korin's not going to cause us any trouble. I thought we were past that."

On another day, Korin might have found that funny. "I'm not the problem he's talking about."

Varajas lowered his sword, looked around. "Where's Ádan?"

"That's the question of the hour," Nikki said.

"Prince Lysander approached me and asked about him. Said he hadn't seen Ádan for weeks. And Nikki said you haven't seen him either. And I've only seen him a few hours at a time, maybe one night in three."

"Could he have gotten himself in trouble?" Nikki asked.

"It's Ádan," Varajas answered in a dry voice. "So of course."

"The Blades are back in town." Nikki rounded on Korin. "When was the last time you saw him?"

"Just last night. And he's been...different. Quiet. Tired all the time."

Varajas grabbed a towel from the edge of the mat and began drying himself off. "He's been a little off since he got back from Ulek. Whatever he saw down there, I think it really spooked him."

"And he's been talking more to that fucking tree," Nikki grumbled.

"No," Varajas corrected. "He's been trying to get the tree to talk to him."

"It doesn't?" Korin only just caught himself before he said *she*.

Varajas shook his head. "You ask me, I think it's better that way. Grandmaster Derian—he used to talk to that thing and it would talk back and I tell you, you've never seen a more haunted man."

"But if that were what Ádan was obsessing about, he'd be here, because this is where the knife is," Nikki pointed out.

Varajas turned a searching look on Korin. "Has Ádan talked to you about...I don't even know. Magic? The knife? Trying to figure out how it works, what it is?"

Korin shook his head and hoped he didn't look too guilty. "I asked him—after you all found me with the cultists, I told him I didn't want to be part of..." Korin waved his hand around to indicate the safehouse. "He seems to have taken that to heart."

"Oh yes." Nikki was outright glaring now. "We're not supposed to sully your delicate little soul with our scary magic. Last time Ádan talked to us—and this really was the last time we talked, now I think about it, we discussed strategies. About maybe finding a wizard who *could* help us understand the magic better."

"Ádan didn't like that idea," Varajas added.

Korin hoped that was still true because…his mind was churning. Surely Ádan couldn't have… "I have to go."

"Go where?" Nikki asked suspiciously.

"I may know where Ádan is. I hope I'm wrong, but…if I'm right…either way, it wouldn't be safe for you."

Varajas accepted the statement. Nikki still looked like he didn't trust Korin, but there wasn't anything Korin could do about that. He left them both in the safehouse and head out into the city. Hoping against hope that he was wrong.

---

22

*K*ORIN WAITED ON the road, far enough away from the house he couldn't be seen, close enough he wouldn't miss anyone coming or going.

He waited all afternoon and well into the night, but he didn't abandon his post. And finally, as the half moon rose into the sky, his wait was rewarded. If anyone could say that being right this time was a reward.

Ádan was on the road coming away from Loukanos's mansion.

Ádan saw Korin and hesitated. After a pause no longer than a breath, he straightened his shoulders and walked up to him. "What are you doing here?" he asked.

"I think that's my question."

Ádan took Korin's arm and drew him along, walking them both away from the mansion. "It's none of your concern what I'm doing."

Even as he'd waited, Korin had hoped he was wrong, that Ádan's recent absences had a different explanation. He'd swung back and forth between frightened and furious, betrayed and confused, and now all those feelings whirled together in a tangled mess. "Are you working with him?"

Korin half expected Ádan to lie, but Ádan gave an answer that had to be the honest one. "He's teaching me magic." He still sounded exhausted. And now more than a little defeated. "You shouldn't be here, Korin. It isn't safe."

"It isn't safe for you either. *He* isn't safe."

"My life hasn't been safe since the day my father handed me over to the knights. And I have a duty." Ádan's hand slid down to tangle his fingers with Korin's, but Korin pulled away.

"You can't trust him." Korin didn't even want to say Loukanos's name out loud.

Ádan managed a tired smile. "I know. Believe me, I know the game I'm playing. But it's all right. This is what I was made for. And maybe this is what Derian intended for me all along."

Korin stopped, turning to face Ádan. "He's a terrible man. He's dangerous. You can't go back there."

"I don't have a choice. I need to learn what he has to teach. There's no other way to do this."

"I could—"

Ádan put his fingers over Korin's lips, silencing him. "No. Don't even think it. You shouldn't—I never should have dragged you into this. I never should have..." His eyes—his whole face—had a hollow, haunted look. He moved his hands down to Korin's shoulders, gripping tightly even as Korin tried to shake them off. "Listen to me. Please. After everything that's happened, after... after everything, I can't stand the thought of anything happening to you. Especially if it happened because of me."

Korin's anger drained away, leaving empty fear in its wake. "I don't want to see anything happen to you either."

"Korin. Sunshine." Ádan brushed one hand back through Korin's hair. "I've been a coward. And selfish. And I've known— I've been thinking about this for a long time, but I couldn't bring myself to say it."

The fear twisted in Korin's stomach. "Ádan..."

"You have such an amazing future in front of you. You're brilliant. And kind. And so good inside. And you've found your place, I think, and someone who can teach you."

Korin's insides lurched. "You knew…about Sheluna?"

Another tired smile. "I keep telling you I'm a spy. You must not think I'm a very good one."

"I'm sorry. I was going to tell you, but…"

"Shhh." Ádan continued to stroke Korin's hair. "It's all right. It's more than all right. You found something that's for you, something that makes you happy. I know how much you needed that.

"In the end," he continued softly, "That's your world. That's where you belong and we both know it."

Korin caught Ádan's hand. "What are you saying?"

Ádan leaned down so their foreheads pressed together. "You give me hope," he whispered. "You remind me there's a world worth saving. That there are people worth saving. But to do that—to save them—to protect them, I have to walk this path, and I can't bring you with me. If you got hurt because of me, I couldn't take it.

"This burden, I've seen it destroy too many good people. I've lost friends, and people I respected and people I loved. I can't let that happen to you, too."

"Ádan, wait, listen—"

Ádan let go and took a step back. "I'm sorry. I'm sorry I dragged you into this. I'm sorry I let you think…" Shadows reached up and swirled around Ádan. And then he was gone.

Korin heard one last whispered, "Good-bye."

"Ádan!" he yelled. Then again, as loud as he could. "*Ádan!*"

But there was no answer.

KORIN WALKED THE FAMILIAR BATTLEFIELD, except this time it was silent. No cries, no screams; no one begged for help or for release.

The people were still there—knights and soldiers, wizards and priests. They still struggled, still pantomimed pain and fear. But there were no voices coming from their mouths, no sound but the wind blowing over the mountainside. Korin shivered, cold and alone.

He walked towards the castle. Always before in his dreams it had stood in the distance, dark and untouchable, as it had been in life. But tonight, tonight he was making his approach.

Castle Ulek, the home of the knights. The oldest fortification on this side of the Great Divide, equal in grandeur to the Royal Palace of Ritalle in the north and Castle Darkivel to the south. Years of war had darkened its battlements, destroyed its gardens, buried much of its beauty beneath soot and ash and blood, but nothing could hide or diminish its size or stature as Korin approached walls that towered so tall above him their shadows stretched over half the battlefield.

Or maybe that was just the dream.

The gates of the outer walls stood open. A lone figure stood between them, hidden by the darkness so Korin couldn't make it out, didn't know who it was until the figure spoke. This voice, alone of all the people around, Korin could hear. "How could you do this?"

Korin looked back behind him, saw the battlefield had become a mess of dark, creeping brambles. Shadowy branches reaching up from the ground to touch—to capture—every person who had fallen. "I didn't," Korin whispered. "I didn't do any of this."

"You let her in. You let her have me."

The old man was right. Korin *had* given him to the knife. He'd opened them both to her power, and the old man had suffered—would suffer for the rest of his life because of Korin's choice. Because of Korin's mistake.

"I'm sorry. I didn't know." The second part was a lie. Hadn't Korin expected something close to what had happened? It wasn't like he hadn't seen the knife's power—in the blight, in the cultists, in his dreams. But he'd been too eager, too desperate. He'd gambled with this man's life, and this man had paid the price.

What was "I'm sorry" in the face of that truth?

What was he doing here? What was he *doing*? The knife was inside. Everything terrible was inside. The only reason to go in was for Ádan, but Ádan had left him. Ádan didn't want him there.

Korin turned, and another voice—a woman's voice—called out, **Wait!**

Korin wanted to ignore the call, to keep going, to leave all this behind him. But he could hear the pain, the sadness in her voice, and Korin had never been able to walk away from pain.

The pale woman stood at the gate. *You* **don't have to go**, she whispered.

She might look like a woman, but she was no more human now than she had been before. Korin could feel the power radiating from her—the power that infused every horror, every death, every decay that covered the fields surrounding the castle. "I won't help you anymore. I shouldn't have..." Korin looked to the old man who now huddled beside her.

This—Korin realized—this was everything Teriad had warned him about. Unlikely Teriad had known about the knife, but he'd understood the power he saw. Power used by the knights. Power called on and abused by the cultists, and—Korin was coming to see—by his own order. Korin had opened himself to this power when he'd killed those people. In doing so, Korin had become a piece of the cancer. Korin had become a part of this thing that Teriad had spent his whole life fighting against.

If Korin didn't stop, if he didn't turn away now, that cancer would only spread and poison everything he did. Everything he was. Until he became no better than Loukanos. Until Korin became no better than the most toxic of the knights.

So he looked the woman in her crystalline, gray eyes and said, "I'm done with you."

I know he left you, she answered. **I know how that tears at you. But that's no reason to leave me.**

Korin's heart twisted at the thought of Ádan. But he kept his voice steady. "This isn't about him."

I want to help him. I want to help both of you. But Ádan— he doesn't belong to me.

"Neither of us belong to you. I'm not yours. You can't have me. I *won't* have you."

Her voice rose. **He's in danger. He's vulnerable and I can't help him.**

"You can't help anyone. You can only destroy them."

Korin—

Korin turned his back on her and began to walk away.

Korin, please. Don't leave me. Don't leave me here alone. It's so dark and there's no one—please, Korin, come back! Her voice became increasingly frantic as he kept going. **Please don't leave me alone.**

Korin broke into a run and her cries faded behind him. He ran and ran and ran. Until the dream fell away and he returned to the deeper darkness of sleep.

23

*K*ORIN HAD LOST track of the time, so he was startled to see how long the shadows had gotten when the knock on his door startled him out of his reverie. He stood up, absently noting his body's stiffness. He'd been sitting still, in his chair by the window, for a very long time.

He opened his door to reveal Marta standing there, arms crossed, as stern a look on her face as he'd ever seen. "You know what time it is?"

Korin glanced out the window again—he didn't keep any sort of timepiece in his room. "Almost dinner, I guess?"

Marta rolled her eyes. "Dinner was two hours ago and change."

"Did I miss..." Korin couldn't think of an ending to that sentence. It wasn't like anyone in the house required anything of him for dinner. "Is there something you need?"

Marta came into the room and closed the door behind her. She took the chair by the window—the only chair—and gave Korin a careful look up and down. "You know what day it is?"

Now she'd asked the question, Korin realized he didn't. Yesterday had been...no, not yesterday. The day before, or maybe the day before that? When had he and Ádan argued? How many days had it been?

"That wizard from the palace—boy with the bat—he came asking about you again. So I thought maybe it was time you and I had a talk."

Samir, she meant. Which made no sense. Korin had sent the message to Sheluna that she wouldn't see him for a couple days. No reason for her to send Samir looking for him. Unless… "How long has it been since I went out?"

"Over a week, now."

"That can't be right." It wasn't possible. Korin would have noticed that much time—that many days spent doing nothing but sitting in his room, staring outside, trying not to think.

He sat down heavily on his bed. Fell back against the wall. A week? "I just needed some time to…" To what?

"This about that noble boy of yours? The pretty one? The girls have noticed he hasn't been by asking about you."

The old fear of discovery rose up, but it was a pale and hollow feeling, not strong enough to even stir Korin to move. "Yes," he answered, rather than argue. Because it was true and not true. This was about Ádan and more than Ádan, but Ádan was the easy part that anyone could understand. "He doesn't want to see me anymore." That was the first time he'd said the words out loud, and his throat tried to tighten around them, to take them back.

Marta sighed. "Ah, Korin. How old are you?"

"Twenty-two," he answered automatically.

"You don't even know how young you still are. Which I know doesn't help. When I was your age, last thing I ever wanted to hear was that things would look different when I was older. But anyone could see how head-over-heels you were for that boy, and I know how much that can feel like it's everything."

That was the trouble, Korin wanted to say. If he'd had the energy, he could have explained that it would have been all right if he and Ádan *had* been everything. But there was the knife and the war and Sheluna and Loukanos and Derian and Teriad and all the rest of the world that had come between them.

And all that Korin could understand rationally, and he could put the pieces together and understand how they all fit, but deep down inside, at the hollow core of himself, none of those words mattered. "I want him back."

"Course you do. That's how it goes."

"What can I do?" Surely there was a solution to this problem. If only he could get his mind to wake up from this sluggish bog it had been in for—apparently—days on end.

Marta gave him a long, appraising look. "If he walked away, there's not much can be done about that. His choice and all."

And that was the answer Korin knew. The answer he'd been trying not to think about.

But Marta's tone gentled as she continued. "But this is the thing you learn with age and experience. Sometimes, with time and patience, absolutes don't look so absolute. Sometimes fights happen and we say things, and then we realize later that maybe those things are less important than we thought."

Except there hadn't been a fight. That, Korin might have understood. There was just…Ádan walking away.

Marta was still watching Korin intently. "Wish I had something better to tell you. Truth is, sometimes love is enough and sometimes it isn't. And heartbreak is part of life, but you can't stop living because of it."

How many heartbreaks before Korin got to be done? How many people were going to send him away?

"One thing I can tell you true," Marta went on, "you're not going to feel any better if you keep just sitting in here and doing nothing. I let that go on long as it needs to, but it's time you got back to occupying yourself. If you go downstairs, the girls'll find you some food. But first—and I can't say this strong enough—it's time you took a bath and put on something you haven't been wearing for a week."

Korin blushed, embarrassed. "I didn't realize…"

Marta rolled her eyes again. "This is why you need looking after." She pushed out of the chair. "I'm going back downstairs. I expect to hear a report that people saw you out of this room."

Korin didn't know what to say. Other than, "Thank you."

Marta waved the words away and left.

KORIN BATHED. And changed. And ate. Verania and Holli were quiet as they worked around him, cleaning and closing down the kitchen in between running drinks to customers in the still-busy bar. Holli flashed him a quick smile when he looked up and met her eyes, and Verania squeezed his shoulder walking by. Silent comfort.

The food made Korin feel much better. How long since he'd eaten? How much of his hunger had he been ignoring—even suppressing—with unthinking magic?

After he finished, Korin slipped out the back, into the darkening streets. He needed to walk, to stretch. He needed to think.

The city was at its most awake and alive at this hour, when day was turning to night. The streets were loud and crowded, but Korin moved through them with an easy confidence he never would have imagined when he'd first arrived here. The noise, the bustle were, themselves, a shield, and Korin had come around to the realization that no one was paying any more attention to him than he was to them. He, his wizard sigil and wizard self, just blended into the background like everything else.

No breeze tonight, but Korin had the trick, now, of adjusting to the steamy weather and felt as cool and comfortable as if he were back in the south. In just a few short weeks, he'd learned so much from Sheluna. How much more was there to explore? How much more magic was there to find?

Teriad would have warned this path was dangerous. And maybe he had a point. It was Korin's curiosity that had drawn him over and over again to listen to the knife, to touch its power, and in the end, to break a man who had come to Korin for healing. He'd trusted Korin and Korin had used him—let the knife use him —and now an innocent had paid the price for Korin's mistake.

Like the people Korin had killed. Who hadn't been innocent, but they'd been helpless against Korin's magic. They'd had a right to be angry, to be terrified, and Korin hadn't needed to kill them except he'd let himself be driven by his own fear and bad judgement.

Bad judgement that Ádan didn't seem to even believe in. When he talked to Korin, when he talked about Korin, he made it sound like Korin could do no wrong. Flattering as that was, Korin knew better. And that belief—Ádan's conviction of Korin's saintly nature had led Ádan to walk away to protect him rather than let Korin decide what risks he was willing to take.

Sheluna's way. Teriad's way. Ádan's way. How much longer was Korin going to let himself be led around by other people? How long was Korin going to stumble forward before he found his own way?

A way that was moving forward because he wanted to, not because he was afraid of what was behind him. A choice, a belief, a goal. Something he understood, rather than stumbled into or fell back onto out of habit.

It was time. Korin needed to take all these parts of himself— the good he'd done, the mistakes he'd made, the people he'd loved, and the choices that had brought him here—and figure out how they integrated into a whole.

Unfortunately, while that decision was easy, the answer he sought was not. Korin wandered long into the night, lost in his thoughts, and had moved no further towards finding his path by the time he came home, exhausted, and collapsed into this bed for the first good sleep he'd had since Ádan had left him.

24

THESE WEEKS HAD been the worst of Ádan's life. No good could overcome the presence of Loukanos and the absence of Korn.

Ádan had done this to himself. He'd made his choice, and it certainly wasn't the first time he'd had to live with hard consequences. Even on the worst day, he was still in a better place than Derian or King Kolyn or any of the other men and women who had died in Ulek. What right did he even have to complain? He was alive and whole, and no amount of his own personal suffering would clear the ledger of what he owed those people.

All the same, it was a misery living with Loukanos. Ádan was now certain the wizard needed neither food nor sleep. With Ádan here nearly all the time, the wizard responded with annoyed impatience every time Ádan insisted he needed either of those things.

Loukanos was sharp, cruel, petty, and vicious. But he was also brilliant, and Ádan was discovering in himself an aptitude for magic he'd never before had the time to explore. In its own way, that made everything worse. Because when Ádan wasn't miserable, he was ecstatic.

When Ádan did sleep, he was haunted by nightmares where

Derian and Korin both hung, rotting, from the Ulek ramparts. Or from the tree. Sometimes they spoke to him. Told him it was his fault. His failure. Sometimes they said nothing, but stared at him with cold, dead eyes. Ádan recognized the guilt that drove these dreams for what it was, and determined the price one he was willing to pay if it kept Korin safe. If it kept Korin free of all of this.

Ádan wasn't free, but when in his life had Ádan ever been free?

Today he was tucked in the corner of the study, on one of the only unstained chairs in the house, watching Loukanos work his way through a complicated ritual. Ádan watched the flow of energy as Loukanos carefully wove it through the body under his hands. Ádan watched every shift, every pulse, every line. He'd seen enough of Loukanos doing magic on corpses to work past his revulsion and actually focus on what Loukanos was doing.

This wasn't too far off from when Korin healed people. It was that same sense of reaching through the body for the memory of some past state. Except this person was dead, and as far as Ádan had seen, even Loukanos couldn't bring people back from death.

It sometimes seemed like he might be able to. As Ádan watched, rotting skin regrew. The body filled back out. Not alive, but it took on a sheen of health. As the ravages of death fell away, Ádan could see what had killed this man: a knife wound through the gut. It grew more and more pronounced as the magic contin-ued, until it started bleeding, as though it had just happened.

The tendrils of Loukanos's magic wrapped through the man, tight and squeezing as Loukanos put a hand over the man's eyes. "What did you see?" Loukanos murmured. The magic flared, and the corpse took a breath.

Ádan held very still, hardly daring to breathe himself. *Could* Loukanos bring someone back from the dead?

"What did you see?" Loukanos demanded more insistently, as his magic flared brighter.

The corpse let out a long, low groan.

Then collapsed into mush on the table.

Loukanos pounded his fist in the oozing remains. Ádan tried not to gag at the sight. Before he'd come here, he thought he had a strong stomach. He thought he'd seen every horror, that nothing could still affect him.

Loukanos spun to glare at him. "How long have you been there?"

Fortunately for Ádan he had progress to report. Loukanos was at his most dangerous when he'd failed at something. "I have the research you wanted. About the blight." He held up the bound notebook he was carrying.

Loukanos stalked over and grabbed it out of Ádan's hand, heedless of the blood and viscera he was smearing on the cover. He flipped through the pages where Ádan had painstakingly recorded every relevant detail and observation he had found in journals, articles, and treatises scattered through the library of the Balance.

Ádan was proud of the work he'd done. Loukanos had wanted evidence of the blight, or the power that drove it, and Ádan had despaired in the beginning because he knew—he *knew*—that evidence would only exist in Ulek and here, and that Loukanos would be able to read into that the existence of the knife, even if he wouldn't know exactly what he was looking for.

What Ádan hadn't taken into account—what he hadn't even thought about until he stumbled over an old Flame wizard's journal talking about a monstrosity that had attacked him in the wilderness—the cult. The people who had tried to kill Korin. Who had been spreading the blight in Triome.

Once Ádan knew what to look for, Ádan found hints and clues of their presence all over the continent. Most focused in Ulek and around this city, but Ádan had cherry-picked his data and assembled a report that made it look like the knife's power was spread everywhere.

That was the only way in which he'd massaged the information. Other than that, he'd copied observations and thoughts and experiments with absolute integrity. Because if the conclusion wasn't going to be pointing right at Triome as a hiding place, Ádan wanted to know Loukanos's thoughts. If anyone could analyze and explain the cult—or maybe even identify the true nature of the knife—it would be this man.

As he read, Loukanos's anger and frustration seemed to drain away. He wandered over to a chair, still focused on the notebook in his hand, and sat, flipping forward page after page.

"Interesting," he murmured. And gave Ádan a long, considering look. "What did you get out of this?"

Ádan had already put together his answer to this question. It had to be carefully constructed. He couldn't afford to play dumb—not only would it defeat the whole purpose of why he was risking himself like this, but Loukanos would see through it. On the other hand, he couldn't give away that he knew too much. "There's definitely a…power, of some sort. It's too consistent, too widespread. Something the wizard orders aren't tied to, and don't seem to know about at all."

"A power…yes." Loukanos looked back down at the notebook, flipped forward some more. "Tell me, Ádan, are you a religious man?"

Ádan didn't follow the change of topic. "I don't go to church, if that's what you're asking."

"But do you believe in the divine? The Shepherd and the Prophet. The Light watching over us."

"I don't know," Ádan answered honestly. "I've had other things to think about."

Loukanos nodded, as though that was the answer he expected. "The church and the knights have been in opposition for years. It's no surprise there wasn't a great focus on matters of faith in your ranks. And of course, before the knights existed to distract them, the church and the Brotherhood spent a great deal of time harassing wizards. And with good reason. The nature of our studies and practices means that, as a group, we look within for power, rather than without. It makes us no friend to the church."

Ádan still wasn't sure where this was going. "Whether or not there's a God, the church is a creation of people, prone to corruption as much as—"

"Yes, yes." Loukanos irritably waved Ádan's argument away. "My point was not to argue about politics. My point is…belief. If one is willing to accept the presence of divinity, then does it stand to reason there might exist divinity's opposite?"

Ádan raised an eyebrow. "You're talking about evil? In a spiritual form? There are some who might say you fit that label."

"And some who might say the same of you, if they knew the truth of your background. But finger-pointing and petty fears don't make anything more true."

Loukanos was talking about the knife, about the idea it could be more than just a creation of magic. "So your idea is that this… opposition—this divine evil—is responsible for the blight? For the people who've mutilated themselves? For…" he caught himself before he let too much slip. "For everything?"

Loukanos didn't answer. Instead, he spread the notebook on the table and gave a flick of his hand towards Ádan. "Leave me to study. I'll summon you when I have use of you again."

Relieved, distressed, Ádan left.

25

ORIN SLOWLY STROKED his hand along Cír's flank, feeling deep into the Tiger's body, memorizing every fold of muscle, every pulse of his breath, every tiny capillary. Cír pressed into Korin's palm, rumbling his approval.

"You see how he fits together?" Sheluna asked. She was watching from her chair on the other side of the workroom, close enough she could step in if Korin somehow upset Cír, but far enough to give Korin space to work.

"He's beautiful."

"You see what I mean? More like us than not."

Korin was certainly having no trouble identifying how everything fit together, how all the systems inside the Tiger matched up with systems inside humans and firstborn. "I can see how I'd heal him, if he were hurt. You're right, it's not much different. Once you know the patterns to look for." He opened his eyes, grinning, and gave Cír a deep scratch behind his ears to thank him for his patience.

Sheluna watched the exchange, her eyes glowing like banked embers, thoughtful. "Have you considered that we might find you a familiar? You'd learn the binding magic easy enough. Most of it you already know."

"I'm not a Wing wizard," Korin answered automatically.

"I'm not asking you to be. I only meant..." She sighed and held out her hand. Cír rolled to his feet and padded over to press his forehead into her palm. As always, Korin marveled that something so big could move so quietly.

Sheluna leaned down and pressed her cheek against the top of Cír's head and asked. "Do you know why the orders exist, Korin?"

Every wizard knew why the orders existed. To train, to police, to guide. But Sheluna never asked a question where the answer she wanted was obvious. "Is there something more than I think?"

"Always," she answered with a little smile. "To every question, there's always a deeper answer."

"So tell me."

She lifted her head and Cír settled at her feet. "Once upon a time, long long ago," Sheluna's eyes burned brighter with amusement, "my noble ancestor Kormanth zhi Darkivel was born."

Korin knew that name. Every wizard knew it. "He created the orders."

She nodded. "He was a genius. I've read his journals, and I can tell you that he had an understanding of magic far beyond anything you or I will ever accomplish. Have you ever seen Castle Darkivel?"

"I've never been there."

"Someday I'll take you. You should see it. It's beautiful."

"I've seen paintings. And heard stories. They say it's the greatest castle in the south."

"Kormanth built it in a day. He literally raised it from the ground, and sculpted it with nothing more than his power and his imagination."

That...Korin couldn't even imagine how that might be possible. "That sounds like a family story that's grown in the telling."

"And yet, we have the records of multiple witnesses to the

event. It happened. And I'm telling you this so you understand when I say that Kormanth had power and skill like no one who has ever lived, I'm not exaggerating."

"Okay." Korin still wasn't sure where this was going.

"And yet, Kormanth was a teacher. Reading his accounts—he took more joy in the tiniest accomplishments of his students than he did in any grand display of his own. He believed that anyone with the slightest talent, the barest temperament for magic should have the opportunity to learn. And he understood, in a way few people of natural brilliance and talent ever do, the true challenges of learning.

"Kormanth created the orders—only five to start with, but they expanded to nine, and then, of course, the Knights fractured off to form their own order, but now we're back to nine, and I expect we'll stay here for a while. He created the orders so there would be a natural subdivision of magic, a limited skillset that any individual wizard has to learn. And for most wizards, that's a blessing. Think about it, Korin. Think about the people you went to school with. How many of them struggled with even the most basic lessons?"

Sheluna ran her own school, so of course she knew the answer. "Most of them."

"Exactly. For most, it's a ten-year course of study to earn their sigil—to reach the point where they get to apprentice and start learning the real magic of their order. And for most of those, apprenticeships last for years, and they still never learn more than the most basic bag of tricks. And that's fine. Because even a little magic, mastered, is still extraordinary.

"But you and I, Korin—wizards like us—the structure fails. You're so young, and yet you took in everything Teriad knew to teach you. You picked up bits and pieces of Crystal knowledge just from being in that school for seven years. You've internalized everything I've given you, and come up with a couple of ideas along the way I never would have thought up on my own."

This was certainly tempting—flattering—the concept that he was too good for limitations, for the rules. But that seemed like a dangerously seductive line of thinking. "Why wouldn't he just say that? Why not build this into the system if his plan was for smart wizards to be free to learn anything?"

"I can't tell you how many times I've wished I could ask him." Sheluna spread her hands, gave a frustrated shrug. "But I think it just never occurred to him people would limit themselves. He saw the orders as a starting tool, not a line that, once drawn, no one should cross."

She gave him a soft smile. "I understand this goes against so much that you've been taught. But…you've got so much potential. So many years ahead of you. I hate to see you limit yourself."

"Why?" A part of Korin hated himself, but it was a question that needed to be asked. "I'm sorry, because you've been nothing but kind to me, but I have to wonder—"

"What I'm getting out of it?"

Korin blushed at Sheluna's blunt phrasing, but that was exactly it. He nodded.

She didn't seem upset. Only tired. She sighed. "Give yourself a few more years, and you wouldn't ask that question. Live a life surrounded by wizards who can't look beyond their own limitations…or who won't. What you bring me, Korin, is a challenge. A new perspective. You're someone I can talk to, share ideas with."

"Surely the other Archwizards—"

Sheluna cut off that thought with one raised eyebrow. "Like Loukanos, you mean?"

"Well, not him, but…"

"But who?" Sheluna shook her head in slow negation. "I won't bore you with a list of their failings, but suffice to say, the rest of my colleagues are uninterested in sharing secrets or becoming friends."

It occurred to Korin that maybe that should be a sign. If everyone else in the world disagreed with Sheluna…

But maybe sometimes everyone else in the world was wrong. Wasn't that the lesson he'd learned from Ádan?

"I need to think about this."

"Naturally." The glow in her eyes softened and faded as she leaned back in her chair. "Although it seems like you've been thinking a lot of things through, lately. I don't feel like I've had your full attention for weeks."

"You haven't," Korin admitted. "But it's...there was a..." Again, that urge to hide. But if he couldn't trust Sheluna with the truth, what was he doing here? "Ádan and I broke up."

"Ah." One word that spoke volumes. "I'm sorry. Well then. Go do what you need to do. Just remember, lovers come and go, but magic is yours, always."

26

*Á*DAN SANK HIS awareness into the body on the table. Loukanos had brought it in as a corpse, but he fed it with false life so Ádan could practice.

He was following the blood on its complicated path, feeling it pulse and flow, learning the byways of veins and arteries and capillaries. Power was useless without understanding. Derian had been the first to explain that to Ádan, and Loukanos had echoed it back many times over the past few weeks. Magic was useless unless its wielder understood the thing he was trying to affect. To change.

Ádan was starting to build a map when Loukanos said, "Tell me about Naktigan."

By now, Ádan was used to this trick—Loukanos trying to distract him, break his concentration. He liked testing Ádan, and —if Ádan failed—punishing him. The punishment was always couched as another lesson. How would Ádan understand pain he never experienced?

The first time had been a shock, and it had almost shaken Ádan out of his pretense, had almost goaded him into fighting back. But he'd kept his head, reminded himself of his mission. And he'd learned. He took the pain, studied it every bit as much as Loukanos said he should. Going forward, he'd improved his focus, got better at not being rattled by interruptions.

But this wasn't a question Ádan had expected, and it almost pulled him out. "Naktigan?" he repeated softly, buying time as he settled the magic into a place he could keep it moving without a lot of active thought.

"Yes. The night of the slaughter. The power Derian used to make it happen."

Despite his best effort, Ádan's concentration wobbled. This subject…what did Loukanos know?

Tiny needle-pricks of power rippled over Ádan's skin. "Do we need to have this lesson again?" Loukanos asked in a too-kind voice.

Ádan took a deep breath, forced his mind back to the magic. Cold calculation, that was all he could afford right now. He couldn't let himself think about… "Were you there? At Naktigan?"

"I was in proximity. Not close enough to see the ritual as it was taking effect, but I felt it. The raw power of it. I felt the deaths. And afterwards, I saw the results. All the dead."

Ádan heard the smile in Loukanos's voice, knew he didn't dare open his eyes or it would be too much to maintain his careful mental distance. But still, a flare of anger made him say, "Including two of your own."

"Did Korin tell you that?"

Cursing himself, knowing that had been a mistake, Ádan remained silent.

But Loukanos went on breezily. "Ah, yes, Teriad and that other apprentice of his. No great loss, and if it gave the people an outlet to drain their anger, so much the better. Teriad's own fault for letting himself get captured. But what I'm more interested in is the magic that came out of Ulek. What exactly Derian did. How did he summon it, control it?"

If Loukanos thought he could goad Ádan into an emotional corner where he'd have trouble telling a smooth enough lie, then all the better for Ádan. Because it wasn't going to happen. "I don't know. Naktigan was the night I ran."

"Oh?" More curiosity than disbelief in Loukanos's tone, which was good.

"It was chaos inside the castle. Surely you can imagine. There had been talk for weeks of mutiny—whispers in corners. You understand. The King and the Grandmaster had a death grip on their authority to keep it from crumbling. And then that night... I felt...something. It put everything inside me on edge. It did that to everyone. And suddenly no one was watching me. So I got out."

As Ádan spoke the words, he made himself believe them. He wouldn't let the truth form itself in even the deepest depths of his thoughts.

Needles against his skin; tiny, sharp points of pain. It didn't hurt enough to be a punishment. This was merely Loukanos's frustration. He said nothing more, and after a moment, he left, and the pain faded.

Ádan let go of his own magic and collapsed back into the chair. That had been dangerous. Loukanos's questions were getting close. Too close. Ádan still had so much to learn, and he didn't have the tools to figure out the knife, but it seemed time to start figuring out an exit strategy.

For right now, though, he had to get out of the house. He needed an escape and a chance to breathe.

It probably said something very wrong about Ádan that the place he went to look for peace was the Academy ruins. The safehouse would have Varajas and Nikki, full of questions Ádan didn't want to answer. The ruins were a haunted graveyard, but they were quiet and no one was going to wander in off the street, so they were a refuge of sort.

Even if there was still the tree. Even if there were still the bodies hanging off the tree. Derian and Korin were there, and had been joined by others. Ádan recognized King Kolyn. Two others were strangers—an older man and a young woman. Their skin was charred and blackened. They'd burned to death, but the sigils of the Staff that hung around their necks were clear.

"What do you want from me?" Ádan demanded of the shadowy tree that probably wasn't even really there.

Now, as before, he received no answer.

A footstep behind him made Ádan jump. He was wound so tight he almost yelped, but he bit back the noise and turned to see Varajas standing there. "Dammit, V, I came here to be alone."

"Well I guess none of us get what we want these days."

Varajas didn't look like he'd been getting enough sleep lately. His dark copper skin had a sallow cast that wasn't just about the way the Academy twisted the sunlight, and his shoulders slumped down noticeably inside his dark shirt. But his eyes were sharp as they focused on Ádan.

"I talked to Lysander," he said. "About our idea to send people to the south to look for survivors."

Ádan looked up at the tree, at the bodies swinging in a nonexistent wind. "I'm not so sure now that's a good plan."

V went on like he hadn't heard. "Lysander has to go anyway. King Kolyn is dead, and it isn't like Prince Calimar will be allowed to take the throne, so every noble in the world is asking who gets to take over Ulek. It's going to be complicated. But it's as good a cover as we're likely to get. So I'm going to go with him."

"You shouldn't go. It's too dangerous."

"Is it?" Varajas paused, waited until his silence forced Ádan to look at him again. "What's dangerous, Ádan? Because I look at you standing there, practically hypnotized by that…thing, and I think the danger isn't waiting for me in the south."

This was too much. After constant mental duels with Loukanos, his own sleepless days and nights, the magic…Korin… Ádan had nothing left for this argument.

And Varajas seemed to see that, because his tone softened.

"Besides, with Ruan in the city, it's dangerous for me to be showing my face on the streets. Hoping if I'm gone for a while, by the time I get back, he'll have moved on."

Ádan couldn't find anything to say to that, and after another moment, V went on. "If there are others, we need them. Even a few would make a big difference. The three of us—if we're all that's left—it's not going so well. I know you can see it too."

"I'm trying my best, V." Ádan's voice sounded whinier than he'd meant.

"I know." Varajas put a hand on Ádan's shoulder. "I'm not criticizing. You weren't prepared for this. None of us were. But this is what we have now, and we're going to need to find a way forward."

Ádan looked back at the tree. The tree that refused to speak to him. "If we fail…"

Varajas shrugged. "Then we'll probably be dead, and when the world goes to Hell, it'll be someone else's problem."

If Varajas meant that to be comforting… "You're no help."

"You've got to get some distance from it, A. Choices made out of desperation aren't usually the best. You have to find a way to think about this like it isn't the end of the world and figure out what the good decision would be if you had real options." He pulled his hand back and also looked over at the shadowy tree. "That's what Derian said to me once."

"If I had real options…" Ádan shook his head. "When was the last time we had options? Ten years ago? A hundred?"

Varajas was quiet again for a while. When he spoke, his words were careful. "I know how you felt about Derian. But if you ask me, he wasn't good at taking his own advice. He didn't look at the options; he just kept pushing us forward in the same direction the Knights had always gone, hoping something would suddenly change. That the world would treat us differently.

"Options, Ádan. We need them. Which is why Nikki and I have kept our distance from this dangerous game you're playing with the Archwizard. Which is why I'm going to Ulek. Which is why you're not going to stop me."

Ádan nodded, conceding the point. "Be careful."

"Of course."

Varajas left as quietly as he'd come. Leaving Ádan alone with the tree, with the bodies.

Ádan approached it, moving in close to stand beneath Derian. For the first time he looked, really looked, facing full-on the rotting, mutilated corpse of the man he'd worshipped. It was hard to think, to talk, around the throbbing, leaden lump in his gut, but Ádan forced the words. "I'm failing you."

So hard to admit. So hard to stand here, taking in the sight that had been haunting his dreams for weeks. "I'm failing you and I don't know how to fix it."

This wasn't a dream and the bodies on the tree were only shadows. Derian had no response. Would never say anything again.

Something tight and hot loosened within Ádan at that thought, at the thoughts he'd been avoiding for weeks—months. At finally facing it, saying it out loud. "You trusted me with this. You put me in charge. But I have no idea what to do, or how we succeed at anything but postponing the inevitable."

Options, V had said. What options could there be? The Knights were dead.

But Ádan wasn't. Varajas and Nikki weren't. So what could they do?

Ádan was too tired for any brilliant revelations, but in a strange way, he felt better. Facing Derian, admitting that everything was going wrong—it felt like a start, not an end.

And he'd been away long enough Loukanos would probably be wanting him again. Time to go back.

AND YES, in fact, as soon as he walked in the door, Ádan heard

Loukanos's voice summoning him upstairs. "Coming!" Ádan yelled back.

"Where have you been?" Loukanos asked irritably as Ádan came into the study. The Archwizard was surrounded by books and hand-written notes, but the space on the table before him was taken up by a wide, flat, polished sheet of crystal.

"Out." When Loukanos was in a mood like this, there wasn't a correct answer, so Ádan aimed for short.

"Yes, out. Where you so often go." And incredibly, Loukanos smiled. "And there it is," he murmured.

"There what is?"

Loukanos waved a hand and the door behind Ádan slammed shut. "So very well done, Ádan." Loukanos's smile grew. He sounded eerily happy.

Ádan took a couple steps back. He couldn't help himself. Every instinct was screaming to flee from the monster grinning that rictus smile. "What did I do?"

"You fulfilled our bargain. Oh, I know you didn't intend to. But here you are."

Ádan still wasn't sure what Loukanos was talking about, but he was beginning to suspect. What he did know was that standing here, puzzling it out, was a really bad idea. He kicked a chair at Loukanos and spun for the door.

Except he didn't.

The chair hung in the air, frozen in space nowhere close to the Archwizard, and Ádan stood frozen too, stopped mid-turn by his body simply shutting down.

"You think I didn't know the game you were playing? You think I didn't suspect?" Now Loukanos sounded disappointed. "And you were playing so well. A shame to blind yourself to something so obvious."

Loukanos came closer, moving into Ádan's view. "If it makes you feel better, you sold the lie. At first, I did believe you. That you'd abandoned your people, run away when you could. So that was well done. I'm not often fooled."

He reached up, traced a finger down Ádan's face with the same calculation in his eye Ádan had seen directed at body after body. "And then you went *out*, and came back to me reeking with power. Soaked in it. The same power you claimed to know nothing about."

Ádan held panic away by sheer force of will. It wouldn't do him any good. He couldn't afford it right now. What he needed was focus. The same iron focus Loukanos had been teaching him all this time. If he could fight back against this magic…

Pain blossomed inside him, a flurry of explosions he could feel ripping through his body. Loukanos shook his head. "No more magic for you, I'm afraid." He released the binding that held Ádan frozen and Ádan collapsed to the floor.

"I'd like to thank you for leading me to the Academy. I'd looked there, of course. And well done on whatever magic you have hiding the power source from anyone who would look. But you were close to it, weren't you? You touched it. And I know that's where you were."

The tree. He meant the tree. The knife. He knew. Or thought he did.

Because the knife was below, deep below. Even knowing to look in the Academy wasn't enough.

Was it?

Ádan needed to—

Loukanos clenched his hand and Ádan's insides ripped and shredded and all coherent thought was driven away by screams.

"The most fun, of course," Loukanos said conversationally, "would be to leave you like this on Korin's doorstep. To force him to watch you die. But I can't trust that he wouldn't be able to save you. So I'll have to do the next best thing and leave you here. I'm afraid it won't last long. For which I apologize. You've been a good servant and you deserve more of my attention than I can give you. But I don't dare delay the opportunity you've given me."

He paused at the door. Ádan could barely make sense of his words through the pain. "You'll be dead when I return, of course. But I promise I'll do something worthwhile with your body. I owe you that much."

And then he was gone, and Ádan could do nothing but spiral deeper and deeper into the white-hot agony of his body tearing itself apart.

27

HE CLIFFSIDE PARK belonged to Prince Lysander, but he didn't seem to visit it often. Ádan had brought Korin here once, and it seemed as good a place as any for Korin to think.

Below, Triome spread out like a beautifully crafted model. To the east, the docks reached their long fingers into the glittering blue ocean. To the west, strands and pockets of civilization reached into the jungle. To the north, it stretched further than Korin could see. The bright colors and patterns of rooftops and flowers that had so startled Korin when he'd first arrived now looked like home.

He'd spent most of the day at Marta's, engaged in healing. The work had been easy, relaxing, and—most importantly—distracting. It had given him a break from the questions that had been swirling in his head for days now.

Teriad would have approved of the work. Teriad, who believed Korin's efforts were best directed as Teriad's had been, healing anyone who came to him. Person by person, life by life.

Teriad had believed that every life mattered. He'd focused their work on the people who had no other resources, no one else who could help them. Who couldn't afford the doctors or wizards who charged huge sums of money for their skills.

Korin believed in that mission. He, too, wanted to help everyone he could. But the trouble was, he was only one wizard. Even if he healed every person who found him, who knew to come to him, there would still be suffering, sickness, death all around.

Sheluna, now, she was all about the big picture. She had grand, sweeping ideas. Blue sky magic—pushing the limits of what they understood, of what they could do. How much potential was there? How much could Korin accomplish if they worked together, challenging each other? Could he find new ways to help people? Magic that wasn't limited by one-on-one?

But if he threw in with Sheluna, what else would he be signing up for? She hadn't spoken of it directly, but Korin knew her ambitions. She wanted him to challenge Loukanos. To become an Archwizard himself. To give her an ally with which to reshape the world.

The last thing Korin wanted was to be dragged into another war. The last thing he wanted was to be put in a position where he was forced to kill another person. And he was afraid that was where any path with Sheluna would eventually lead him.

Frustrated, Korin pushed his hands back through his hair and fell back onto the grass. The same circles in his mind. Over and over, back and forth over the same ground. And it was getting him nowhere. If only—

Korin!

It was good he was lying down, because the paralyzing force of the voice in his mind stopped everything. For a moment, he couldn't even breathe.

When he finally gasped a breath again, it was enough to grit out, "Leave me alone!"

Korin, you must help! He needs you. Now.

Her voice held a mix of command and panic. Korin could feel

it like his own fear. He scrambled to his feet. "Who needs me?" he asked, certain he already knew the answer.

Images flooded his mind. And Korin took off at a run.

KORIN FOLLOWED the knife's directions through Loukanos's gruesome house, taking the stairs up two at a time. He slammed the study open and immediately spotted Ádan on the floor. Ignoring the horrifying detritus that filled the room, Korin rushed to his side and dropped to his knees beside Ádan.

Ádan wasn't moving, but his body was twisted and curled in on itself in clear agony. A hand on Ádan's chest reassured Korin that he was still breathing—albeit shallowly. A blink into his other sight told Korin the rest.

Ribbons and veins of magic ran all through Ádan, constricting and twisting and tearing. Destroying him from the inside out. What Loukanos had created—this was more than just a simple attack. Along with the magical energies with which Korin was familiar, he'd laced the power of the blight—of the knife—to make it feed and grow, and…something else. An element Korin couldn't identify.

Not that he was going to waste time trying to figure it out. Ádan remaining life would be measured in heartbeats if Korin didn't do anything. Korin lay a hand on Ádan's forehead, the other on Ádan's chest, and reached inside.

The blight was the easy part. Korin shattered that power with a single focused effort. Loukanos's magic was clever, but by tying the blight into his own energy, he'd stopped it from getting its usual firm hold. Korin banished it with the ease of familiarity, undiminished by the weeks since he'd fought it.

Ádan's heart stuttered, threatened to stop. Korin sent a thread of power to squeeze and release, forcing it to keep going, grateful now for the work he'd done with Sheluna. He was going to have to split his focus between keeping Ádan alive, banishing Loukanos's power, and putting Ádan back together. A few months ago, he wouldn't have been able to do that. Today…

They would see.

Korin reached his awareness through Ádan's body. The last time he'd done this—but no, he couldn't afford the distraction of memory. Just the thankfulness that Ádan was so familiar to him, that he knew the rhythms and flows, how Ádan should feel, which made it easier to identify the tendrils and laces of energy that didn't belong.

Loukanos was powerful and skilled. The magic flowed all through Ádan, invasive and deep, with little barbs of power everywhere to keep it attached. Unthreading it was going to take care and time that Korin wasn't sure he had.

Korin wove his own power against Loukanos's, wrapped it in bonds of his own making. He couldn't remove it yet, or even stop it, but he could blunt its fangs, slow it down while he brought Ádan back.

Except even there, Loukanos was a step ahead of him.

Healing Ádan should have been the easiest part. The destructiveness of this magic meant that it moved fast, that the change had been quick and intense—exactly the sort of thing that made healing easy. Ádan's body should still clearly remember being healthy.

The extra power that Korin hadn't been able to identify—now he knew. Somehow Loukanos had broken Ádan's body's connection to its own past. He'd made it forget, erased everything that came before. Korin didn't even know how that was possible. It was a change, not just to Ádan, but to reality itself.

This was Loukanos's power, and it made Korin despair. How could anyone fight this? Loukanos had made healing impossible. Had gone out of his way to make sure Ádan would die in a way Korin couldn't stop.

And why? What had Korin done? What had Ádan done?

Except try to exist. Try to help people. And Loukanos came along and...what gave him the right?

Loukanos's power pulsed against Korin's restraints, trying to finish its job. Korin drove all other thoughts, all the panic and hopelessness, from his mind and focused. He refused to just give up. He refused to let go.

"You can't leave me," he whispered fiercely. The words he should have said before. "I refuse to let him take you from me."

But what could Korin do? He could hold Ádan in this state of dying, keep him from falling any further. He could pull away the strands of Loukanos's magic bit by bit. But he couldn't heal Ádan. He couldn't bring him back.

Could he?

Korin had been under Ádan's skin. He'd touched every part of Ádan with his magic. He'd healed Ádan. He'd pleasured Ádan. If he could remember—if he could dig deep into his own mind, his own power, could that be enough?

Korin flooded Ádan with power. He had to work fast. He couldn't afford to second guess himself—not with this. Instinct and memory wove together with the skills Korin had spent years perfecting. And all the while, another part of his mind worked inch by inch through Ádan to clean out every trace of Loukanos's power.

He lost track of time, of everything that wasn't Ádan. Nothing was left but magic and the struggle to fix what Loukanos had broken.

Until...

Korin pulled back, realizing several things at once. First, that he couldn't feel any remaining trace of Loukanos's power. Second, that Ádan's heart was beating on its own. Third...

Ádan's eyes were open, looking up at Korin. His lips moved, but no sound came out. He took a deep breath, tried again. "Korin? What are you...? How...?"

Korin put his hand against Ádan's cheek, feeling equal parts exhausted and triumphant. "He doesn't get to take you from me."

Ádan reached up and grabbed Korin's arms to drag him down into a crushing embrace.

28

*A*S KORIN LAY wrapped in Ádan's arms, pressed tight to Ádan's chest, he listened to Ádan's heartbeat. Felt the rise and fall of Ádan's breathing. Rhythms that had become familiar to Korin, part of the world as it should be.

The relief that filled him drained away, replaced by furious anger. "You don't get to do that," he spoke into Ádan's chest. "You don't get to do that! You don't get to leave me."

Ádan's gentle fingers stroked down his cheek, brushing away tears Korin hadn't noticed himself crying. And Ádan, usually so glib, said nothing.

But he didn't let go.

Korin could have stayed here forever, wrapped in Ádan's arms, except as the adrenaline faded and Korin's mind started working again, he remembered where they were. And that it wasn't safe. He pulled back and Ádan let him go enough that he could sit up and ask, "Where's Loukanos?"

And that set Ádan into motion, struggling to his feet. Korin followed the movement, grabbing Ádan's hand to reclaim his attention. "*Where?*"

"He was going to the Academy." Ádan's calm voice belied the frantic look in his eyes. "He knows about the knife. I have to—"

"*We* have to."

Ádan took hold of both of Korin's hands, pulled him around so they were facing each other. "I can't ask that of you."

Korin squeezed tight, stared directly into Ádan's eyes. "You're not asking. I'm telling. We do this together, or not at all."

A hint of a smile played at the corners of Ádan's mouth. "You're not leaving me much choice."

"None."

Ádan nodded, serious again. "Then let's go."

They ran across the city. The whole time, Korin was listening, straining his mind to try to reach for the knife. Always before, she'd spoken to him. She'd established the connection. He'd never asked—never thought he might need to speak with her.

But she would know if Loukanos was there. She would know what he was doing. She would know if they were already too late.

If Loukanos found her, if he got his hands on the power Korin had always felt—the power Korin had refused—there would be no end to the horrors he could wreak.

As THEY GOT close to the Academy, Ádan grabbed Korin's sleeve and pulled him to a stop. Ádan lifted a finger to his lips, gesturing for silence, and Korin's skin prickled as Ádan's magic pulled shadows around them. Hand in hand, they crept forward. And as they crossed through the gateway, Korin's heart sank.

Loukanos was there, standing in the center, before the shadow of the tree. At his feet writhed Varajas. As Korin refocused, he could see the strands of Loukanos's magic sunk deep into Varajas, torturing him.

"Tell me where it is," Loukanos demanded and closed his hand into a fist. The magic similarly clenched and Varajas screamed.

"I can feel it, the power. So close. Just tell me where it is, and I'll let you die."

Korin looked sideways at Ádan, whose expression had gone murderously cold. "You have to get Varajas out of here. When I get Loukanos's attention, grab him and get away."

"You can't fight him alone. He's an archwizard."

Ádan had a point. But Korin wasn't alone. And they didn't have time for Korin to explain. "Loukanos knows you. He'll be able to sink his power right back into you, unless you've figured out how to stop that somewhere in the last few minutes. I can't protect you and fight him all at the same time. And..." Korin paused, steeling himself to speak the hard truth. "Whatever happens, he can't get the knife. You know that as well as I do. If I fail, you have to get it away from here."

Ádan grabbed Korin by the back of his head, dragged him into a desperate kiss. He pulled back, just as sudden, leaving Korin gasping. "Go," he said.

Korin straightened and stepped forward. He felt Ádan's magic slip away, and he called out "Loukanos!"

The archwizard didn't turn. "Hello, Korin. I wondered when you'd show up." He squeezed his hands into fists and Varajas screamed.

Korin couldn't break Loukanos's power—not when he'd had time to sink so deep into Varajas—but he could do the next best thing. He wove a line of energy around Loukanos's magic and Varajas passed out.

Loukanos gave a disappointed sigh. "Very well. If you want to talk. Let's talk." He turned, raised his hand, and now it was Korin's turn to scream as the bones of his feet erupted out through his skin and drove into the ground, pinning him.

"It's such a pity Teriad got to your first. Ruined you." Loukanos twisted his wrist and Korin's legs crumpled. "Such potential, wasted." He squeezed his fingers into a fist and Korin couldn't breathe, his lungs refusing to expand.

Loukanos's power was like iron. Korin had healed himself through war, blighted magic, and blighted cultists. He'd spent weeks with Sheluna honing his understanding, his will. And even so, Loukanos's magic had locked into him, taking control as easily as if Korin's body belonged to him.

Help me, Korin thought, turning pleading eyes towards the tree.

He wants me. You do not.

Korin focused on breathing, willing his body to remember how. Power, will, conviction. Korin was able to wrest back enough control to take a gasping breath before Loukanos's grip tightened once more.

He's cruel. He creates suffering. He causes pain. That isn't what you want.

He'll use my power. He'll set me free.

"It's your turn to answer questions," Loukanos said, walking over to Korin. "And I'll make you the same promise. A quick death —an end to your suffering. Tell me where it is. The power of the knights. Because I think you know."

The pain was too intense. Korin couldn't keep his eyes open. He couldn't see if Ádan had gotten Varajas away yet. But at least he didn't seem in any danger of losing Loukanos's attention. Korin would have laughed, if he could. But all he could manage was his hand clawing helplessly at his throat.

"I'm sorry," Loukanos said in a silky voice. "Did you have something to say?"

The pressure on Korin's lungs let up. Korin dragged in enough air to say, "Go to hell."

His lungs snapped closed again and now his skin started to burn. The new agony reawakened the pain in his legs, his feet, which had started to dull. *He's going to kill me. Like he almost killed Ádan. Is that what you want?*

No. But she sounded unsure.

She didn't like being locked away. She wanted to be free. And she was lonely. All that much, Korin had figured out. Her power corrupted everything she touched. It was the knife's power the cultists had touched. The knife's power, flowing through that old man, that had almost killed him even as Korin had tried to heal him. Korin couldn't promise to set her free. Not as Loukanos undoubtedly would. So what could he offer?

Loukanos's power snapped and Korin's magic, freed of all resistance, washed through him in a wave of relief. He opened his eyes to see a dagger stuck in Loukanos's shoulder, and Loukanos focused on something over Korin's shoulder.

"Well, well," Loukanos said as he reached up and pulled the knife out, tossing it to the side. "More resourceful than I thought."

Ádan stepped up next to Korin, grabbed him by the arm and pulled him to his feet. "V and Nikki are below," he whispered. "They'll do what needs to be done. I couldn't leave you."

"How sweet." Loukanos raised his hands again. "You can die together."

Korin struck. He reached directly for Loukanos's nerves, burst energy through them. Loukanos flinched, but didn't lose control. Korin's power was pushed out, reflected back and Korin had to cut off the energy before he was incapacitated by his own magic.

Ádan was circling around and did something to draw Loukanos's attention. Korin took advantage of the distraction to heal himself, then tried to reach in and grab Loukanos's lungs the way he'd done to Korin.

But Loukanos gave an idle wave and Korin was knocked back down. He pointed at Ádan, and Ádan stumbled. Even the two of them together were no match. But Korin had known that going in.

He just wants to use you. He doesn't care about you. He doesn't care about anyone. All he wants is power.

And what do you want?

To learn. To help people. Korin looked over at Ádan. *To be with him.*

You don't want to be alone. Just as I don't want to be alone.

Was it that simple? Could it be that simple? *I can't set you free. I can't let you hurt people. But I can promise to listen. I can promise I won't walk away again.* It was a risk. Talking, listening—leaving himself open for the knife's manipulation. But Korin had trusted Ádan, had trusted Sheluna, when all good sense would have told him to do otherwise. Look where that had gotten him.

In the end, if everything was going to go wrong, Korin wanted it to be because he had chosen trust. Not because he had walked away from it.

The branches of the tree reached for him, and Korin felt the power of the knife flowing into him. It pushed all the remains of Loukanos's influence from his body and filled him with a crackling energy that threatened to explode out.

Korin focused. He had to keep control. "Together," he said through gritted teeth.

"What?" Loukanos asked, turning to face him. "What do you mean—"

Korin sent the knife's energy through Loukanos like a spear, shredding Loukanos's defenses and driving him to the ground. Writhing tendrils of energy shot through him, wrapped around him, held him down. Loukanos struggled, but all his power was nothing next to the knife. It broke against the deadly spear like a wave against rocks.

Ádan looked at Korin, eyes wide. "What did you do?"

Korin ignored him, advancing on Loukanos. "She doesn't belong to you. And neither does Ádan. And neither do I."

"You arrogant little whelp," Loukanos snarled. "You can't—"

Korin twisted the magic, took away Loukanos's ability to speak. "My turn now. You're done." He reached through the arch-wizard, sending his magic into all the places the knife had opened. "I'm not going to kill you. Even though you probably deserve it. More than anyone I've ever met, you deserve it. And you can thank the fact that Teriad "ruined" me. In fact, you should just take some time to think about the fact that you owe your life to him.

"But take that time elsewhere. Somewhere very far away. Because I don't want to ever see you again."

Korin reached in deeper, to Loukanos's very center and up, until his magical strands were resting in Loukanos's brain. "But I can't just let you go. Not like this. Because even if you don't come back after me, and the people I care about, you'll just keep hurting people. And I can't have that."

Korin thought at the knife. *You know what I need. Can you do it?*

I can. Yes.

Then do it.

Loukanos screamed as the knife's corruption moved through his brain, twisting as it went. "I'm taking away your magic, Loukanos. You don't get to be a wizard anymore."

Loukanos writhed as the knife worked. Korin had known this was possible, but usually it was a punishment handed out by the entire council of archwizards, and it took that full council to accomplish. Terrifying that the knife had the power to do this all on its own.

Korin shivered at that thought, but he didn't tell the knife to stop.

When it was done, Korin released Loukanos from the magic that had been binding him. "We're done with you now. Get out of our city." He turned and walked out of the Academy. He didn't look back.

29

KORIN STOPPED OUTSIDE the Academy, hearing Ádan's footsteps behind him. "Just how long have you been able to do *that?*" Ádan asked.

Korin couldn't bring himself to look Ádan in the eye. "There may be some things I haven't been telling you."

Ádan's hands landed lightly on Korin's shoulders. "Yeah, well… call it even?" Korin gratefully leaned back into him and Ádan's arms slid around him, holding him tight.

They stood like that for a long moment, as Korin's heartbeat slowed to something approaching normal and the stress of the fight faded. Until Ádan broke the silence. "We should check on V. And tell him and Nikki the threat's over." He pulled back and turned Korin to face him. "Is it over? You let him live."

"I pulled his fangs. He won't be able to do magic anymore. It's over."

Ádan studied Korin's face. "You called on the knife. She talks to you."

"For a while now, yes."

Korin waited for censure, for accusation, for horror. But all Ádan said was, "Okay." And took his hand.

They went into the safehouse. Korin saw to Varajas, undoing the damage Loukanos had done. Nikki was upset with Ádan, with the secrets he'd been keeping that put them all in danger. V was quieter, and, after Korin was finished, simply said that he was still planning to go south, and they'd all talk about this when he returned.

Nikki wasn't happy with that answer. "You're just going to let—"

Varajas interrupted him with a shake of his head. "There's no *let* here. There are no rules. No order. We're going to have to figure that out. But we won't be able to do that until we know—for sure —that we're the only ones left."

"I'm sorry," Ádan said, subdued.

"I know. You did what you thought was best. But you did it without talking to anyone, and maybe you should take some time to figure out why you're still keeping secrets when there's just three of us left."

Ádan said nothing. It was only after Korin had finished and the two of them had sought privacy in Ádan's room that he spoke.

"They hung Derian's body off the main gate and left him there to rot. I haven't been able to get it out of my head. I see him in my dreams. I see him..." He fell back onto the bed, staring up at the ceiling. "I just keep thinking that will be you. Or V. Or Nikki. I just thought if I could keep you safe—if I could keep all of you safe—that would..."

"Would what?" Korin asked softly when Ádan trailed off.

"I don't know." Ádan draped his arm across his eyes. "I don't even know what I thought would happen."

Korin sat down next to him, put a hand on Ádan's thigh. "I got hurt by plenty of things before I ever met you. You can't keep me safe by staying away. But maybe, together, we can look out for each other."

"I led him here." Ádan pulled his arm away, looked up at

Korin. "I thought I was being clever. I thought I was a step ahead of him."

"He's an archwizard." *Was* an archwizard. Loukanos wasn't going to get to hold onto that title much longer. "And you've been —Light, Ádan. Have you even had a real night's sleep since you got back from Ulek?" Korin reached up with his other hand to brush gentle fingers across Ádan's temple and back into his hair.

Ádan caught his hand, squeezed it. "I almost died today. I would have died, and Loukanos would have taken the knife. And everything Derian asked of me, expected of me, I would have failed."

"Because you tried to do it alone," Korin said, scolding as kindly as he could.

Ádan sat up, leaning into Korin so their foreheads rested together. "I never should have pushed you away like that."

"And I should have told you from the start about the knife. You were trying to look out for me, and I was the one who said I didn't want to be part of your mission."

"Do you still feel that way?" Ádan asked softly.

Korin rocked his head side-to-side in a no. "I've been giving this a lot of thought. The knights, the knife—this is part of who you are. I can't draw a line between you. Yes, bad things were done by the knights, but...I've made my own mistakes and it's hypocrit-ical of me to try to say it's different. From the start, you've said you don't understand the knife, and the more she talks to me, the more I think...maybe there's actually something there to understand. I want to help you. I want to be *with* you. In every way."

Ádan's bright smile broke free—the one Korin had been missing for weeks. "So is this the point where we kiss and make up?"

"Please?"

Ádan pushed Korin onto his back, took Korin's face in his hands, and kissed him hungrily, and Korin was flooded with weeks of pent-up wants and needs and desires. He wrapped his arms around Ádan's waist, pulled him down so that Ádan's entire body was pressed against him.

Korin had needed this. He needed it never to stop. He needed this to be forever. "Don't leave me like that again," he whispered against Ádan's lips.

"I won't. I swear I won't. That was the worst decision I ever made."

"I'm not—you can't protect me by hiding things from me. You can't keep me safe by walking away. You keep me safe by staying with me. And I'll keep you safe the same way."

"Together," Ádan murmured back. "From here out on. I promise."

Later, they would have to talk about the knife. They would have to talk about the future. Varajas was going out to look for more knights and whether he found them or not, each possibility brought its own complications. But for tonight, they were safe and they were together.

For now, that was more than enough.

ÁDAN KNEW what he had to do. And that he had to do it alone.

They had promised *together* and Ádan meant it. There was just this one piece of old business that had to be taken care of. After, he would tell Korin. He would make the full confession. No more keeping secrets. But Ádan didn't want to argue about this, or listen to Korin's reasons why Ádan shouldn't be here.

In this one time, in this one case, Korin would be wrong.

Ádan crept up the stairs, wrapped in shadows. He made no sound. When he reached the study, he found the door open, and Loukanos inside. The wizard's back was to him. Whatever Korin had done to break Loukanos's magic, it had worked. Before, Ádan hadn't been able to breathe in this house without Loukanos knowing. Now, he had no idea Ádan was there.

Korin was willing to trust that Loukanos would remain harmless, that fear and respect would keep him away. Korin saw the best in everyone. Even this creature. Ádan liked that about Korin, and never wanted him to lose that faith. On the other hand, Ádan also believed it was his job to protect Korin—and the world—from monsters.

Ádan didn't understand what Korin had done, what he and the knife had changed in Loukanos to take away his magic. Korin seemed to believe it was permanent, the change he'd wrought. But it was a big world full of plenty of magic none of them could even anticipate, and smart as Korin was, he couldn't see every possibility. None of them could. Which was why Ádan wasn't willing to trust that Loukanos wouldn't come back.

The simple truth: Loukanos had to die.

But he wouldn't do this from behind. He wouldn't stab Loukanos from the shadows like some back-alley assassin. The wizard would know who killed him. And why.

"Hello again," Ádan said.

Loukanos stiffened, then visibly schooled himself. He turned to face Ádan, no particular concern on his face. "Hello, Ádan. Come on Korin's bidding to make certain I leave the city as he ordered?" He sneered the last word.

"Korin doesn't know I'm here."

Ádan let that sink in, saw the dawning awareness in Loukanos's eyes.

"Korin may trust that you're harmless, but I don't. I can't let you leave. I can't risk what would happen if you ever got your power back."

Loukanos spread his hands. "You'd kill a helpless old man?"

"Yes." Ádan spread his own hands, showed they were empty. "And I'll do it with the very magic you taught me."

Ádan vividly remembered how it had felt when Loukanos had set off the magic inside him. The twisting, ripping, tearing. The pain. His fingers curled into claws; he focused energy as he'd been taught, reached inside the monster standing before him, and ripped Loukanos's insides open.

Ádan made it quick. Partly because he didn't feel like listening to any last words Loukanos might have to give him, any empty threats or warnings or pleas. But also because, despite everything, Ádan couldn't find it in himself to torture the man. Even this man. Cold-blooded murder was far enough over the line.

Loukanos collapsed to the ground, gasping. His eyes rolled back. His heart fluttered and skipped. Ádan felt every tortured breath, every fading heartbeat. Until there was nothing more. Loukanos was dead.

The house was still. Until the voice spoke in Ádan's head, feminine and powerful. **Welcome, my darling. I've been waiting.**

ABOUT THE AUTHOR

Growing up in a house that included a library of thousands of science fiction and fantasy books, Barbara J. Webb had no choice but to become a writer herself.

A midwesterner at heart, Barbara has lived in Missouri, Kansas, and Arkansas, but finally settled in only two blocks away from the house in which she was born. She enjoys her small-town life with her husband and her cat, and occasionally dreams of keeping horses. Or even better, unicorns.

In addition to writing, Barbara enjoys cooking (her chocolate chip cookies are always in high demand), crochet, and video games. She's been an avid role-playing-gamer since she was ten. Like most of her family, Barbara began music training when she was very young, and has played violin with the Columbia Civic Orchestra, the Missouri Symphony, and several local bands.

Find more of Barbara's books and news at
barbarajwebb.com

Sign up for her newsletter at
buttondown.email/bjwebb

ACKNOWLEDGMENTS

I wrote Twisted Magic because I needed a break. I was stalled out on other books, and had lost touch with the joy of what I was doing.

I sat down and decided I was just going to have fun. I was going to start at a beginning and write to the end, and try not to second guess myself along the way. Twisted Magic was what came out.

This was the first time I'd permitted myself to add the romance into the fantasy, and I loved it. I had so much fun with Korin and Ádan, their love story and their world, that I immediately started work on the next book, this one you now hold in your hands.

Books take a lot of time and energy, and I want to thank those writing friends who have kept my spirits up along the way: Kij Johnson, Lane Robins, Kevin McNeil, Luke Tolvaj, and Dominic D'Aunno. Also thank you to my CSSF and Novel Architect work-shoppers, and the Repeat Offenders, for reminding me every summer why I love writing.

FURTHER READING

**The story of the Knights continues in
TWISTED SECRETS
Book 3 of Knights of the Twisted Tree**

Releasing June 2025

Read on for an excerpt.

CHAPTER 1

*S*heluna had an excellent view of the palace courtyard from her rooms, and all week had been watching the preparations for Lysander's forthcoming trip back to Ulek. It made her a little homesick. Not for Ulek, of course. She could cheerfully go the rest of her life without returning to that place. But for her own castle in the south.

Between the war and the politics that had followed, it had been almost two years since Sheluna had been home for anything but the briefest visit. Now it looked like she was going to be stuck in Triome even longer, since the symbol of the Staff had gone suddenly dark in the inner chamber of the Council of Nine. The Staff had lost its leader, and none of the other archwizards knew how or why. No wizard of the staff had, as of yet, stepped forward to claim the title. Disorganized and scattered as the lot of them were, it was possible none of them even knew.

Except for the wizard who had killed him, of course.

Sheluna hadn't asked Korin if he knew anything. If he wanted to talk, he would, and she didn't want to test the limits of their developing friendship by forcing him to lie. Still, she had her suspicions. More power to Korin if they were true.

Cír's ears swiveled towards the door just a moment before the knock came, and Samir's voice on the other side announced, "It's me."

Sheluna twitched her hand, sending a tiny burst of power to open the door. Samir came in, tilting his tall staff down to clear the door without dislodging little Krys. "You wanted to see me?" he asked, righting the flying fox's perch and closing the door behind him.

"Before you left, yes." Sheluna took in the young wizard standing before her. Poised and comfortable in her presence, healthy and calm, he'd come a long way from the terrified, angry creature she'd first met.

He was going south with Lysander. He was doing it for her. Sheluna knew how big a step he was taking, and that she didn't have words enough to thank him. "I have a present for you."

His eyes lit up and a bright smile turned his face into something truly divine. It had taken two years for Sheluna to see that smile. She never got tired of it. "Is it what I think?"

Of course, he knew. He'd delivered the package to her three days ago, when the trader had come from Darkivel. It had been wrapped, but Samir had seen the note, had seen the name of the artist who sent it.

Still, his delight was genuine, and the reason Sheluna had gone through the trouble. "A new card, yes. I told Brialia I needed it quickly. I didn't want you to go back down there without it."

Without any further suspense, she pulled the card from the top drawer of her desk and handed it to him face-down.

He turned it over and gave a little sigh, which made Krys twist her upside-down head to chitter at him. That got Cír's attention, and he lifted his head to consider the bat before lying back down. Krys noted Cír's look and chittered louder, utterly unintimidated by the tiger.

Familiars.

Samir ignored them both, taking in his gift. "Thank you. She always does such amazing work."

Artists who worked on fate decks were rare. Even rarer were artists who created decks useful to wizards. There were plenty of cards in the world in the hands of those who used them for party games or meditations, and those could be painted by anyone, but to create an object that magic would flow through in the proper fashion took not only an artistic eye, but years of study and a mind tuned to the rituals that were part of the creation process.

Magic-worthy fate decks were expensive, and tended to be passed down, generation after generation. Almost every deck was a mish-mash, with cards replaced one at a time as the wizard could afford, and an artist could manage.

Sheluna could afford plenty, and would have paid ten times the price to make her apprentice happy.

This newest card was The Tower. It wasn't a necessary replacement. There was nothing wrong with Samir's current Tower card other than that it was a plain, traditional image. It held no resonance for him, and magic flowed better through cards to which a wizard felt connected.

This new card, commissioned under very specific guidance from Sheluna, held a beautifully rendered painting of the ruined Castle Ulek. The Tower was a card of failed ambitions, of arrogance punished, and what better representation of that than Ulek?

Sheluna had no fate deck of her own. There were plenty of cards in storage back in Darkivel, but this wasn't, and had never been, Wing magic. Still, it was fun helping Samir craft his own deck into something meaningful to them both.

For five years, she'd taken the best care of him that she could. And now she was sending him into danger. "You don't have to go," she said, not for the first time. "I wouldn't think any less of you for staying."

"Afraid you'll miss me?"

She took his cue, kept her tone light. "Always."

"You've got Korin to keep you company these days. You won't even notice I'm gone."

He was aiming for lighthearted, but Sheluna heard the edge beneath the words. "Samir, you're not—tell me you're not jealous of the time I'm spending with Korin."

"I'm not." That sounded honest. "Well, mostly not. But it's good. It's made me look at things. I realize…I can't hide behind you forever."

"You've never hidden behind me. And I wouldn't have thought less of you if you had."

"I know. You gave me so much. You pieced me back together when I would have…" He trailed off, reached his hand up to Krys, who butted against his fingers. "But it's time for me to figure out who I am on my own. Time for me to walk back into the world without you."

"There are safer first time outings."

"Probably." His smile was faint, but present. "But this is something I can do for you. And after everything you've done for me—"

"You owe me nothing," Sheluna said quickly.

"And you owed me nothing. But you helped me anyway."

"Always. I'm always here for you."

He slid the card carefully into a pocket inside his jacket. "I know. And I'll be back before you know it."

After that, there was nothing more to say, except, "Be careful. Come home safe."

After he left, she returned to the window and watched the chaos in the courtyard for a very long time.

ÁDAN LEANED against the wall by the door, watching Varajas pack. The two of them were alone in the empty, echoing safehouse that every day felt more haunted with the ghosts of every Knight who had come before.

"You don't have to go," Ádan said.

"Someone needs to. We can't have wizards poking around our secrets unsupervised. And who else would you send? Nikki?"

"I could—" He broke off as V stopped working and turned to glare.

"You could what?" Varajas pressed. "Take another responsibility onto yourself? Find a new way to get yourself in trouble?"

Ádan kept quiet and after another moment, Varajas nodded and returned to folding clothes. "It's your own flavor of arrogance, you know," he said. "You and Derian both. This idea that it's your job to personally fix everything."

"I'm just worried about you."

"I'll be fine."

It was what V had been saying for days now. Ever since Loukanos had found the academy and… No. Ever since Ádan had led Loukanos here and the Archwizard had magically tortured Varajas to try to get information about the knife. Ádan could vividly imagine what that had been like, having been in the midst of suffering a similar torture—meant to be fatal—before Korin had arrived to rescue him.

Watching V closely, as Ádan had been trained to do, he noticed the slight shake in Varajas's hands. He'd seen the way Varajas twitched at little noises when they caught him by surprise. Ádan was probably doing a bit of that himself. It meant Varajas wasn't at his best, when he was going out alone, where even Lysander wouldn't be able to help him if he were discovered.

Of course, when was the last time any of them had been at their best?

"Besides," Varajas continued, "if I stayed here, I'd be stuck in the safehouse, useless, as long as Ruan and Father Donatien are in the city. Can't be out on the streets with Blades about who know me."

If the Brotherhood found Varajas, the best case was they'd drag him in and execute him on the spot. At worst, they'd figure out that the fact he was still alive meant there might still be other Knights who escaped Ulek.

"I just wish…" Ádan didn't even know what he wished for. Except a different world. A better one.

"We all do. But this is what it is." Varajas tied his pack closed, lay a hand on it. "Lysander's making me part of his personal guard. It'll give me freedom to move around as much as I need. Plus, it'll keep me close to the wizard. I'll do what I can to make sure he doesn't find anything he shouldn't."

"Just be careful." Ádan knew how useless those words were, but he still had to say them.

Varajas knew too, but he let it go. He shouldered his pack and came over to Ádan, clasping his hand tight. "I'll be back before you know it."

"Light protect you," Ádan whispered.

V's response was a flat smile, and a fluttering movement of his hand towards his neck, quickly stilled. "I don't think the Light looks after people like us. But thank you." And with that, he left.

Valus Donatien considered the man kneeling penitent before him. His uniform was flawlessly pressed. His swords were in perfect condition. Every line of his posture was correct. But still, there seemed an air of rebellion about him.

Or was that simply Valus's imagination? Every report he'd received on Ruan for the past few years had been glowing. His commanders held nothing but praise for him. His work in Ulek had been exceptional.

And yet.

People didn't change. That was Valus's belief, reinforced over and over again by experience. No matter how well Ruan tried to hide it, there was a part of him that had always been insubordinate, and that always would be.

But at the same time, Ruan was—and always had been—one

of Valus's most talented Blades. He excelled at both the physical and spiritual demands of the order, which was rare enough, but he had a quick, perceptive mind on top of the rest. That had gotten him into trouble eight years ago, no question, but when that mind was directed towards the interests of the Brotherhood, there was no one more insightful.

Thus, Valus had called Ruan to this audience, and had told him of the Prince's expedition.

"How long will Lysander be in the south?" Ruan asked.

"It's unclear. The politics are complicated. He's to be Ritalle's voice in the determination of a new ruling family for Ulek. I expect that argument will go on a while, but these politics are not my concern. My worry is the wizard travelling with him."

"Samir of the Wing," Ruan supplied, demonstrating that he, too, had been paying attention to the Prince's plans.

Valus knew Samir. Sheluna's apprentice, he'd been at her side often in the final push of the war.

Because it was his business to know these things, Valus was aware of Samir's history. He knew the depths of Samir's loyalty to Sheluna. He knew that, while Sheluna had been a solid ally during the war, she was ambitious. And in the end, no wizard was to be trusted.

Ruan continued. "Darkivel has sent separate representatives to weigh in on the Ulek matter. Which means there's only one reason for Archwizard Sheluna to be sending a wizard along."

"To investigate Ulek," Valus finished. To try to dig up the poisoned, blasphemous magic of the Knights.

It was good that Ruan had been paying attention. It meant it wouldn't take long for him to get up to speed. "We cannot have wizards poking around down there. The magic the knights used, it tainted the ground, the people, the very air. It needs to die with them."

Ruan nodded in quick agreement. Whenever knights and death were in the same sentence, Ruan was quick to agree.

Perhaps Valus was focusing too closely on a single mistake—a moment of bad judgement that was now years old.

He continued. "This will not be an overt mission."

Ruan nodded. "If this wizard knows the church is there, watching over his shoulder, he will be careful. At worst, the Archwizard could send a different agent to search for secrets, an agent we don't know."

That was Ruan's mind at its sharpest. Quick to see all angles of a situation. It got him in trouble, but it was also a valuable weapon that Valus was happy to turn against his enemies.

"This is why I want you to do more than just watch."

For the first time, Ruan looked up, curiosity on his face. "High Father?"

"Now the knights are dealt with, we must return to our true purpose—keeping watch over the wizards. Archwizard Sheluna has always presented a challenge. The church has a weak presence in Darkivel, and she and her wizards are well insulated by her family.

"Samir presents an opportunity. I want you to befriend him. Enter his confidence."

"You want me to spy," Ruan said.

Valus studied him, looking for any hint of defiance. "I do. You are close to his age. You have a gift for earning people's trust. There is no one better suited to this mission."

Ruan gave a silent nod. Not the most enthusiastic response, but Valus saw thoughtfulness behind it, rather than resentment, the clockwork of Ruan's mind starting to turn.

"I'm looking at this as a long-term investment. If you can build a relationship, I would like that to continue into the future. I wish to maintain the advantage he presents. Do not reveal yourself unless necessary."

"What constitutes necessity?" Ruan asked carefully.

"If he finds something he should not." Valus gave a reassuring smile. "I don't expect that will happen. The castle has been thoroughly searched. There is nothing left to find. He'll come to that conclusion soon enough. All I need is for you to gently steer him away, in a way that lets you remain his friend. Then you may accompany him back here to Triome."

Ruan nodded. "I understand." From his kneeling position, he bowed forward, touching his forehead to the floor. "Thank you, High Father."

"The Light wills and the Prophet guides. Go with my blessing."

CHAPTER 2

The sun hadn't quite lifted over the horizon when Samir made his way to the courtyard, his pack slung over his shoulder and Krys still chittering in annoyance at being disturbed from her usual routine. Samir slipped her a small bit of pineapple from the pouch at his belt, trying to mollify her, but she continued to scold him as she ate.

As he reached the courtyard, he had to slow down to navigate among close-packed men and horses. Samir knew how big the courtyard was and wondered just how many people had to be here for it to be so crowded. A hundred? Two hundred? It seemed the Queen-regent wanted to make a point about Ritalle's strength in the coming negotiations.

Prince Lysander was easy to find, already on his golden horse, his golden armor glimmering softly under the lanterns. As Samir approached, Lysander spotted him, called out to him. "Over here! Raj has your horse."

Samir liked Lysander. But then, as far as he could tell, everyone liked Lysander. The prince had proven himself a hero in the war, and yet in person managed to be thoughtful and kind, putting nobles and commoners alike at ease. They'd spent time in proximity on the warfront, with Samir always next to Sheluna, and the zhi Darkivels and zhi Ritalle's having the friendly relationship they did, but Samir hadn't seen much of Lysander since they'd returned to Triome.

Well, that was about to change. They had weeks ahead of them on the road, where there'd be nothing but time to talk.

If Samir had been traveling on his own, he could have gotten to Ulek much sooner. Almost instantly, in fact. If he'd wanted to show off, he could have opened a gate that the whole train could move through where the palace courtyard would be on one side and the ruins of castle Ulek on the other. But the last thing Samir wanted to do was show off. Or answer the questions that would come up if anyone saw him using that kind of magic.

Off to the side of the prince, Samir found the horse that had to be for him. A tall, black mare with the long limbs and heavy hooves of one of the Ulek breeds. She'd do well in the mountains. On her back, a saddle with a high wooden arch that had been attached to the cantle. It would give a place for Krys to hang as they rode. Once again, Lysander being thoughtful.

Holding the reins was a man wearing the golden lion-marked livery of the prince's guard. Raj, Lysander had said. Who's iron expression did nothing to hide the beauty of his face. He had the dark copper skin and smooth black hair of someone born in Triome. He was also tall, with broad-shoulders and a soldier's solid build. Firstborn, like the prince, like Sheluna, like almost everyone who surrounded Samir these days.

It was perfectly safe and reasonable for Samir to find this man aesthetically pleasing. No harm in looking. The flutter inside him was to be expected, having to interact with new people. It was all right to find this angelic-looking guard of Lysander's attractive. No one had ever been hurt by attraction.

"I'm Samir," he said, summoning the smile he'd honed to perfection.

Raj's expression didn't soften. "I know."

Samir had spent five years teaching himself not to flinch, not to panic when someone glared at him like that. Instead, he calmly reached out to take the reins and said, "Thank you."

Raj didn't answer, simply turned and walked away.

Samir put it out of his mind. No sense dwelling. He turned his attention to his horse, ran his hand down her neck, and reached into her with his magic.

A quick, easy check revealed her to be in excellent health. She was well-fed, well-rested. No soreness, no weak spots, no tension or evidence of stress. She'd be a good companion on the road.

Samir tapped the saddle perch and Krys jumped from the staff to the saddle, grabbing with the hooks of her wings and her toes and climbing to hang from the top, where she stretched her wings wide before wrapping them back around herself and settling in to go back to sleep.

Samir secured his staff, then swung up into the saddle. This was it. For the first time in five years, he was leaving Sheluna's protection. Ready or not, it was time to face the world again.

And any consequences that might still be waiting for him in the south.

IT FELT good to be on the road, away from Triome and all its burdens. Away from the knife. Nothing for Varajas to do but watch the scenery and the wizard he was here to keep track of.

Samir, it turned out, was nothing like Varajas had expected.

On the surface, he embodied the Wing image like he'd stepped out of a textbook. Polished in his manner and presentation, with a smile that was to easy, too perfect, to be sincere. Dressed in finely tailored blacks that were utterly inappropriate for summer travel— and would probably give heat stroke to anyone but a wizard. There was something untouchable about that perfection, like Samir wasn't, couldn't be, part of anything real.

All style, no substance—that was the Wing. As shallow and

status conscious as the nobility they aped. Samir looked to fit that mold exactly as the column had passed out of the city and Samir had trotted forward to ride at Lysander's side. Light forbid, if there was a prince around, a Wing wizard be forced to associate with anyone more common.

Varajas stayed close, riding unobtrusively behind, where he could keep an eye on things, and as the day wore on and Samir relaxed, Varajas was faced with the uncomfortable notion he may have misjudged. Which was unfortunate, because this mission would be far easier if Samir was just another shallow, selfish Wing wizard that Varajas could dismiss with impunity.

First of all, there was the bat. That impossibly adorable bat, with her soft-looking red fur and big black eyes that seemed to be watching Varajas with a surprising amount of intelligence. She hung off her perch, just behind Samir's head. Samir periodically reached up to give her a scratch, and she'd rub her head against his fingers like a puppy. Or she would give a scolding chitter and Samir would slip her a piece of fruit. It would have taken a stonier man than Varajas to watch these exchanges without warming a little to the pair.

Then there was Samir himself. By the end of the morning, his polished, perfect smile had relaxed into something more honest. He didn't say much—no great hardship for Lysander, who could keep all sides of a conversation going on his own—but when he did speak, his words were thoughtful and he seemed comfortable with them. He was neither sycophantic to Lysander, nor did he seem interested in proving how smart he was.

Varajas couldn't help but notice the way Samir's hand kept stealing up to touch his familiar. At first, Varajas had assumed Samir was just checking the bat was still there. Or that it was merely a gesture of affection. But as time went on and Varajas had little else to do but watch Samir, the repetitive movement started to seem more like a reflex, a tic. That it wasn't Samir giving reassurance, but seeking it.

What could Samir possibly have to be nervous about?

The other thing just starting to sink in was how alone Varajas was. This was the first of who knew how many days when he'd be surrounded by people he had to lie to, to hide from. Lysander knew who and what he was, but no one else. Varajas couldn't trust anyone. Not today. Not a month from now.

He hadn't thought about this part of it. He'd been so eager to get away from the city, from the oppressive confines of the safe-house. He'd wanted away from the knife, from Ádan, from the dreams. But at least with Nikki and Ádan—and even Korin— Varajas could be himself. If he had complaints, he could be honest about them. If he had nightmares—about the tree, about being tortured by power-hungry archwizards—he could talk about it.

It occurred to Varajas that this was how Ádan had lived a great deal of his life. Alone in Triome, spying, creating a bolthole for the disaster that Derian had seen coming for years. At that time, Varajas had envied Ádan the assignment.

Now, not even a full day on his own and Varajas was already feeling isolated. When ideas came to him, observations about Samir, or Lysander, or just the country they were riding through, he kept looking for someone to share them with. He'd never in his life not been able to just talk. He hadn't thought to prepare for the fact he wouldn't be able to.

He'd mocked the idea of Nikki coming on this mission— volatile, honest Nikhil, who hardly had a thought that didn't pop out of his mouth. It hadn't occurred to Varajas that maybe he was every bit as ill suited to life under cover. As evidenced by how badly he wished Ádan were here right now so Varajas could share this revelation with him.

Too late to turn back. All that was left was to get through it. And it was still better than hiding in the safehouse.

Probably.

Worth it if he could keep nosy wizards out of their secrets. Nosy, good-looking wizards, who made little chittering noises at

their adorable familiars, and whose real smile seemed to be something slow and fragile that stirred a place deep inside Varajas to
wonder if he could coax it into something brighter.

Shit, he was in trouble.

RUAN COULDN'T DENY it felt good to be out of the city. He'd
worried about how long he was going to have to be stationed in
Triome. Being stuck in Ulek, pinned in one place, had been the
reality of the war years. One of the least horrors, but still unpleasant. Ruan had always been happiest travelling.

Prince Lysander wasn't personally devout, but he observed the
forms, which meant he travelled with a priest. On High Father
Donatien's orders, the priest had introduced Ruan as his very
necessary assistant, understanding that Ruan wouldn't actually be
doing much to assist. It gave Ruan a cover that let him travel with
the column, but didn't require him to be in any certain place at
any certain time, so he could carry out his real mission without
interruption.

He was even in disguise, or something like it. He'd packed
away his Brotherhood blacks, donning plain, simple riding
leathers and the sort of light, airy clothes civilians wore. His
twin swords were wrapped in a bundle strapped to his saddle.
The only piece of his true uniform he kept was his prophet's
cross. There was nothing about it that identified him as a
Blade, even if it was a far nicer cross than a priest's assistant
would likely have access to. Ruan simply felt naked without it.

In addition to all that, he'd wrapped his head and face in a
chafiyeh, as he hadn't done since he'd joined the Brotherhood.
There were plenty of soldiers in Lysander's group who had been at
the warfront, and Ruan didn't want to be recognized. He wasn't the
only one of Lysander's contingent dressed this way—Lysander's
crew was a diverse bunch, and a number of them, like Ruan, had

come to Triome from the western desert—so Ruan didn't stand out.

He spent the first day at Dhir, the priest's side. Making certain people saw him there. Dhir wasn't the best company—he knew Ruan was a Blade, and that seemed to make him nervous—but as Donatien had noted, Ruan was good at teasing people out from their shells, and by the time they'd reached the first night's campsite, Dhir was talking easily enough.

Lysander had brought a small army with him, and this many people with horses and baggage meant travel was slow. They had a couple weeks of riding ahead of them. It gave Ruan plenty of time to figure out his approach to the wizard, so for tonight, he planned simply to scout, to get a good look at the man he needed to befriend, but not yet draw attention to himself.

The bustle of getting settled was excellent cover. Everyone was busy unpacking horses and setting up tents and organizing food and water. Ruan flitted through them, unobtrusive and uninteresting, making his way towards the bubble of activity surrounding the prince. That was where Samir would be.

Lysander's campsite was easy to find. A giant, red and gold pavilion was being raised, taller than anything else in the camp. The prince himself stood in front of it, talking to several of his officers. The wizard wasn't with him, but—

Ruan's brain froze.

The man at Lysander's shoulder. It couldn't be.

It was.

He was in disguise, but Ruan knew him. Knew the shape of him, the way he moved the space he filled.

Varajas.

Ruan faded back before he could be seen, trying to make his stuttering brain start working again.

Varajas was here. Varajas was alive. Varajas was *here*.

Ruan's first instinct was to turn and run back to his horse. They were only a day out from Triome. He could be back to Father

Donatien by the morning, make his report, and return with an entire contingent of blades.

No. A visceral burst of rage and his entire body tensed to reject that thought. Varajas was *his*. If anyone was going to capture him, drag him back to the church for the punishment he so deserved, it would be Ruan.

How was Varajas still alive? How had he escaped Ulek's fall?

Probably he ran away, Ruan answered himself in his mind. Varajas was so good at that.

Did Lysander know what he harbored? Was Lysander protecting a knight? These were questions Donatien would ask. This was information he needed. A surviving knight in service to the royal family—Ruan needed to return and report. There was no question where his duty lay.

Except…

Eight years gone and Ruan still couldn't let things go. He couldn't forgive. It was an angry pit in his stomach, a fire that sometimes died down to a smolder, but burned bright and hot at the slightest reminder.

He'd learned to hide it—from his commander, from the High Father, from the rest of the Brotherhood. He'd built a mask of ice and worn it now for eight years, but that didn't keep the bitterness from gnawing away at his insides. It didn't help him sleep. It didn't bring him peace.

Ruan was angry with the Brotherhood, with the church. He was still angry with the High Father, and the choices Donatien had made. He was angry with the world. He was angry with himself.

Most of all, he was angry with Varajas for the decision that had come so easy to him and the actions he had forced Ruan to take. Ruan bore some small sliver of hope that if he could…deal with Varajas, somehow, and douse that spark of fury that lived at the center of this, everything else would fade. He could be whole again. He could be the man he'd once believed himself to be.

There would be no room for error. Ruan wouldn't be able to

pretend he hadn't know exactly what he should do, which was return to the High Father. He would have to wait, and plan, find the perfect moment to strike. In the meanwhile, he would carry out his real assignment. He would befriend the wizard.

But he would watch Varajas. When the opportunity came, he would be ready.

CHAPTER 3

Only one day on the road and Samir was exhausted. The riding itself wasn't so bad—it had been a while since he'd spent this much time on a horse, but he'd be a poor excuse for a Wing wizard if he couldn't magic away a bit of saddle soreness.

No, the exhaustion came from a whole day at Lysander's side, with Lysander's constant conversation. While Samir appreciated the effort Lysander was putting in to make him feel welcome and comfortable, maybe tomorrow he'd make an excuse to spend some time on his own.

Samir looked after his horse, who he'd taken to calling Lady, for her perfect manners. He removed and wiped down her saddle, left the blanket where it could air, and gave her a good, long rubdown. He checked her hooves, her mouth, her legs, both with his hands and then with magic, making sure she was sound. It was soothing work, and Samir enjoyed it.

By the time he'd finished and left her munching on a bag of grain, Samir's tent had been set up. He rated his own private space, which was nice. It was small, a fraction the size of the nearby pavilion that belonged to Lysander, but Samir didn't need much.

Lysander had already retreated into his big tent with Raj, the guardsman. Samir hadn't missed the way Raj had been watching him all day. Did he not trust a wizard so close to his prince? Whatever his problem, Samir hoped he got over it. The staring was uncomfortable.

Samir had known this trip would be uncomfortable. He'd just hoped the discomfort would take a little longer to ramp up. Raj seemed specifically designed by the universe, however, to poke at every sore spot Samir had. The fact that he was watching Samir so closely, when Samir still wasn't comfortable being noticed by anyone—that was bad enough. But Raj was tall, and broad, and brooding, with a handsome face and solid body, and if Samir were as recovered as he wanted to believe, he should be welcoming the attention from someone like that. That he was uncomfortable *because* of all that, rather than in spite of—it forced Samir to face ideas and thoughts and memories he hadn't even realized he'd been avoiding.

Samir wasn't exactly hiding, but it was convenient that he had this tent to himself and that everyone else was tired enough after the first day of travel that he could justify being alone in here without seeming too anti social.

Samir unrolled a blanket and sat down cross-legged, pulling his fate deck from his bag. Krys hooked herself over the rope that ran along the apex, twisting her head to look down at what he was doing.

This was also soothing, shuffling the familiar cards, feeling their solid weight in his hands. He felt the urge to do... something.

Samir recognized what was nothing more than a desire to feel like he was in control. What did he think he was going to do? He wasn't Sheluna, or Korin, endlessly entertained by hour after hour of experiments. He had nothing he needed magic for right now, and using power just for the sake of using power was a start down a dangerous road.

Still, he had the cards in his hands. A simple array, perhaps, to look ahead. It would relax him, and it wouldn't hurt to have a sense of what was coming.

The future was a tricky business. Looking into it was art as much as a science, and notoriously unreliable. Wizards who worked magic through fate decks were considered eccentric at best, even within the Order of the Star. Most wizards turned up their noses at what they considered a parlor trick, nothing more.

Part of the trouble was, people didn't spend the time learning how best to use the cards. They didn't understand divination in general. They didn't understand the ways it could go right and the ways it could go wrong.

Samir had gone to school at the Star. He'd been fascinated with the slippery, intuitive magic. One of Samir's teachers had been an expert, and had indulged all his questions.

He still remembered the day he'd asked about using magic to look into the future. They'd been sitting together on one of the high tower terraces, looking out over the ocean. He'd tracked her down outside of class, and she'd been pleased enough by his interest to invite him up here to talk.

"Take this coin," she'd said, making it dance across her nimble fingers. She balanced it on the back of her thumb, ready to flip it up in the air. "Right now. Can magic tell me whether it will land heads or tails?"

"Of course." Samir had been twelve, and convinced he knew how everything worked. "That's exactly the sort of question you can use magic for. There are only two possible answers."

She gave an indulgent smile and shook her head. "Right there, that's the mistake most people make. They look at the answer, not the question. In this moment, if I ask that question, there's no answer magic can give me. There are still too many variables. How much force will I apply? What direction will I angle it? Or even, will I launch it at all? Those things are all my choice, my action, and magic can't predict it. Not reliably."

With a sharp flick of her finger, she set it spinning up into the air. Then, with a twist of her hand, the coin froze, hovering a foot over the table. "Now the decisions have been made. The coin is in motion. If I ask the question, there's an answer for magic to see. It's all down to force and motion and energy. Predictable.

"Remember that, Samir. The trick of looking into the future is you have to know whether the coin is already spinning, or if it hasn't yet been thrown."

Well Samir was on the road now, no turning back. His coin was definitely spinning. Time to take a look at what was waiting for him.

He was too tired to do a serious casting, but he'd worked with his deck enough it would respond to him even if he didn't have a lot of energy to put into it. He shuffled, clearing his mind, cut, and dealt the top three cards.

The first card down was his just-received present from Sheluna —the Tower. It had broken Ulek—his destination—rendered in beautiful detail. Samir rolled his eyes. Working with the cards it became tempting to personify them, to anthropomorphize magic itself. If Samir hadn't known any better, he'd think this was magic showing a sense of humor.

The pictures mattered. Sometimes, the illustration was more meaningful than the card. Samir's instinct was that this was one of those times.

This was the cards telling him to pay attention. There was something important for him to see.

The following two cards were potentially more illustrative. The deck was divided into suits and powers, and this next was a suit card, the four of air. It bore a picture of two men fighting each other, nearly obscured by the blizzard blowing around them. This card was a warning of forces he couldn't yet see. Of being knocked around by power and influence he didn't know or understand.

The final card in the row was Night, another power, which spoke of deceptions, illusions, and false beliefs.

Neither of those cards were what Samir considered encouraging. For the next row, he needed to pick one to focus on. This entire reading was about Ulek, so no point asking for more information on the Tower. The four of air would be slippery. Not likely to give him a good reading. So he kept his eyes on Night, took a deep breath, shuffled again, and dealt the next three.

This row revealed the Ace of Stone, the Four of Ice, and the Knight of Water. All three were in conversation with Night, modified by its meaning, connected to deception. False faces? Could they be people he needed to watch for? People lying to him? Or something more abstract?

The ace of stone was a guardian. A signifier of responsibility. A person, perhaps, who had sacrificed their freedom for duty. That part could have described Samir himself. He'd certainly come on this mission out of a sense of duty to Sheluna. Except that didn't resonate when he thought about it, and Samir had learned to trust his instincts when he was looking at the cards. He likewise rejected Lysander as the person this card could be pointing to. Lysander had certainly made sacrifices for duty, but he would never be the ace of stone. Lysander was air, or fire. Water at a stretch. The ace of stone would be steadier, quieter, but with a core of beliefs that couldn't be shaken.

Moving on to the four of ice. If it was pointing at a person, it was not a person Samir wanted to be anywhere near. This was a card of corruption of decay, and Samir couldn't forget Night lying above it, adding more deception and lies. This was a warning. Samir just didn't know of what.

The final card, the knight of water. The third of Night's children, this would be another person trying to deceive Samir. Which was too bad, because the knight of water was otherwise someone Samir could imagine liking a great deal. A romantic—someone both intellectual and sensual, an artist or a fellow wizard. Someone with high ideals and the passion to hold to them. If Samir had still been in Triome, he might have thought of Korin. But he couldn't imagine Korin deceiving anyone about anything.

Much as Samir was intrigued by the ace of stone and knight of water, the four of ice was clearly the danger he most needed to watch for, so he focused on that card for the final row. Whatever warning the cards were trying to give, he needed to hear.

After shuffling, he lay out the final three cards one at a time, studying each in turn.

The first was another one of the powers, and not a good one. The Conquerer was staring up at him. A card that spoke of abuses of trust, advantage taken, power stolen without consent. Samir shivered. He knew all too well who that card could be pointing to, and that was almost enough to make him go get on his horse and ride straight back to Triome.

As if the cards heard him, the next card was the reminder of why Samir wasn't going to run away, and Samir's hand hovered over it as he saw what he'd just put down.

On the surface, the knight of fire was a strange follow-up to the four of ice. The knight of fire was fiercely honest, an uncompromising crusader for the good. Not the sort of person who fell easily to corruption.

The fire suit had been one of Sheluna's earliest gifts to Samir, replacing cards that had been over a hundred years of out of date. The face cards were usually portraits of real people, with each suit connected to one of the five kingdoms.

Fire traditionally belonged to Ulek, but given all that had happened, most of of Samir's fire suit now bore the faces of the dead. The king of fire held Kolyn's face, and the wizard of fire was the equally deceased Grandmaster Derian.

The knight of fire was not a face Samir had recognized. He'd asked Sheluna about it, and it had been the first time she had been hesitatant to answer his question. "His name is Arshtar," she finally said. "One of Derian's ranking officers." A knight.

Only much, much later had she told him the rest. That he and Sheluna had been lovers. That he and Sheluna had been in love.

The man on the card was handsome, a firstborn with hair the

color of banked embers and piercing blue eyes. He had fought with Derian, with the knights, against Sheluna and her allies, but he had not been among those who had surrendered, nor identified among the dead.

Arshtar was the reason Samir was going to the south. To find out what had happened to him. To bring Sheluna some peace.

The cards seemed to be saying that Samir would find him. But connected to the four of ice, to Night—that couldn't be good.

Samir spent so long studying the knight of flame, staring at the face of the man he was looking for, that he almost forgot to put down the final card. When he remembered to flip it over, he almost wished he hadn't.

The final modifier to the four of ice—to corruption—was an old card. Neither Samir nor Sheluna had seen any reason to replace it because it was a card that remained the same artist after artist, deck after deck. A traditional image that hadn't evolved for hundreds of years.

A knife with a curved, black blade sat prominent in the center of the card. Surrounding it, overgrowing it, were twisting black branches and dead, black vines. The illustration always made Samir shiver. There was something sinister about that knife, something the artist had done with perspective or shading to make it seem like it was more real than the card, like it was looking for someone to hurt.

The card was Death.

SAMIR OPENED his eyes to darkness. He turned his head to look around and something scratched against his skin, like fingernails against his throat. He didn't scream. The reflex to make noise had long ago been trained out of him. Instead he took a deep breath, sinking into his body. Making certain of himself before he tried to figure out where he was and how he had come here.

He couldn't see, but the rest of his senses were working

perfectly well. It was quiet. Not a peaceful quiet, but the dull, muted silence of death. There were no sounds of people or horses, the endless restlessnesses of a camp at night. No smell of fire or flesh. If the air around Samir smelled of anything, it was a faint, wet rot.

He was lying down, but not on the bedding he'd carefully spread out inside his tent. The surface beneath him was solid and flat—not the soft, but uneven mossy ground he'd gone to sleep on.

"Krys," he whispered, and relief washed through him as an urgent chittering came from above. Krys sounded worried, but not panicked, and Samir adjusted his own emotional barometer accordingly.

Time to risk some magic. Samir called light—a very small light; barely even a candle flame—to the air above him.

Again he had to swallow a scream as shadowy spiders appeared just inches from his face. Another couple breaths and the shadows resolved, solidifying into fingerling branches. A weedy bush. That was what he was lying in. Dead—no leaves. The branches were what had scratched him.

Samir sat up carefully, pushing through the dead bush, to look around at where he was.

A small stone room that had long ago fallen to decay. A single window, high above, showed night outside, stars shining cold and dim in a cloudless midnight sky. Black, knotty roots and desiccated weeds were well on their way to crumbling the walls in Samir's corner. Another nest of roots had broken through the ceiling, as though a tree were growing in the floor above. Krys hung from one of these roots, watching Samir carefully with her sharp, dark eyes. A doorway across from Samir held no door, but all Samir could see was darkness beyond.

What he heard was the scratch of movement. Someone, or something, was outside. Scrapes against the stone. A faint movement of air that could be breathing.

Quiet as a cat, Samir got to his feet, crept towards the door. He held a hand up, signaling Krys to stay where she was. He kept the light steady where he'd summoned it and crouched low, ready to peek out.

When he saw the card.

A fate card. On the floor, in the doorway. It was lying face down, but from the design on the back, Samir could tell it didn't belong to his deck.

He picked it up, flipped it over. A four-sided fortress with a moat, surrounded by fog. This was the four of water. Samir knew this card. He knew all the cards. This one represented blindness, helplessness. An inability to see or stop unseen forces.

Who had dropped it here? Unlike everything else, the card was in pristine shape. It hadn't been here for long.

Outside, whoever or whatever approached was drawing nearer. Samir would worry about the card later. He dropped it...

And began to fall.

ALSO BY BARBARA J. WEBB

The Invisible War

Midnight in St. Petersburg

Inquest

Apocrypha: The Dying World

City of Burning Shadows

What Dreams Shadows Cast

Knights of the Twisted Tree

Twisted Magic